A powerful secret

"Dad," I said soberly. "If I were to ask you to do something really strange, but I said it was the most important thing in the whole world to me, would you do it?"

My father kind of chuckled and said, "It depends on whether it was legal or not, I guess."

I had to grin. "It's legal."

"Then—yeah sure." He brought his arms down and sat up. "If it was really important to you, son."

The grin slid off my face. "Then I need to ask you."

Dad leaned forward, listening.

I hesitated because I knew that once I said something, I could never take it back. And that everything—and everyone—would be changed by it.

"[A] well-written, sometimes gripping story."

—*Kirkus Reviews*

OTHER BOOKS YOU MAY ENJOY

RED KAYAK

Priscilla Cummings

PUFFIN BOOKS
An Imprint of Penguin Group (USA) Inc.

PUFFIN BOOKS
Published by the Penguin Group
Penguin Young Readers Group, 345 Hudson Street, New York, New York 10014, U.S.A.
Penguin Group (Canada), 90 Eglinton Avenue East, Suite 700,
Toronto, Ontario, Canada M4P 2Y3
(a division of Pearson Penguin Canada Inc.)
Penguin Books Ltd, 80 Strand, London WC2R 0RL, England
Penguin Ireland, 25 St Stephen's Green, Dublin 2, Ireland (a division of Penguin Books Ltd)
Penguin Group (Australia), 250 Camberwell Road, Camberwell, Victoria 3124, Australia
(a division of Pearson Australia Group Pty Ltd)
Penguin Books India Pvt Ltd, 11 Community Centre,
Panchsheel Park, New Delhi - 110 017, India
Penguin Group (NZ), 67 Apollo Drive, Rosedale, Auckland 0632, New Zealand
(a division of Pearson New Zealand Ltd)
Penguin Books (South Africa) (Pty) Ltd, 24 Sturdee Avenue,
Rosebank, Johannesburg 2196, South Africa

Penguin Books Ltd, Registered Offices: 80 Strand, London WC2R 0RL, England

First published in the United States of America by Dutton Children's Books,
a division of Penguin Young Readers Group, 2004
Published by Puffin Books, a division of Penguin Young Readers Group, 2006

19 21 23 22 20

Copyright © Priscilla Cummings, 2004
All rights reserved

THE LIBRARY OF CONGRESS HAS CATALOGUED THE DUTTON EDITION AS FOLLOWS:
Cummings, Priscilla, date.
Red Kayak / Priscilla Cummings.—1st ed.
p.   cm.
Summary: Living near the water on Maryland's Eastern Shore, thirteen-year-old
Brady and his best friends J.T. and Digger become entangled in a tragedy
that tests their friendship and their ideas about right and wrong.
ISBN 0-525-47317-3 (hc)
[1. Conduct of life—Fiction. 2. Friendship—Fiction. 3. Boats and boating—Fiction.
4. Death—Fiction. 5. Eastern Shore (Md. and Va.)—Fiction.] I. Title.
PZ7.C91483Re   2004
[Fic]—dc22   2003063532

Puffin Books ISBN 978-0-14-240573-4

Printed in the United States of America

For William

"Truth is always the strongest argument."

—Sophocles

RED KAYAK

CHAPTER ONE

After all this time, I still ask myself: *Was it my fault?*
Maybe. Maybe not.

Either way, I wonder what would have happened if I'd called out a warning. Or kept my mouth shut later. Would J.T. and Digger still be my best friends? Would the DiAngelos still be living next door?

One thing's for sure: If none of this had happened, I'd be out there crabbing every day, baiting my pots in the morning and pulling them in after school. Fall's a great time for catching crabs before the females head south and the males burrow into the mud. I could fix the engine on the boat easy if I wanted. It's not broken like I told Dad. Probably nothing but some air in the lines from settin' there so long. I could bleed the engine tonight, set my alarm for 4 A.M., and be on the river before the sun was up over the tree line.

Don't think it didn't bother me, the way those traps sat all summer, stacked four deep against the back of Dad's toolshed. Some never even got hosed off, they were stashed in such a hurry. Be a lot of work to clean 'em up and rezinc them, too, so they don't corrode. In just a few days, though, I could have four rows of twenty-five sunken pots out there, each one marked with a fresh-painted orange buoy, and all one hundred of those pots soaked and baited with razor clams. Afternoons, I could be hauling in crabs hand over fist, and right now, a bushel of big number-one jimmies would fetch me seventy dollars from the wholesaler—maybe even more, since the price of crabs has gone through the roof.

But this is all so complicated. I can't go back out on the water. Not yet anyway. I can't help it; I keep asking myself, *What if this, what if that?* And then in my mind I see that red kayak . . .

My dad says stop thinking that way. "You be lookin' backward all the time, Brady, you're gonna have one heck of a crook in the neck." He smiles when he says that. But I know what he means deep down, and it's not funny. You can't keep dwelling on the past when you can't undo it. You can't make it happen any different than it did.

My cousin Carl comes over a lot. He's a paramedic and sees a lot of gross stuff, so he knows about getting things out of your head. "Talk it out there, boy," he keeps telling me. "What? You think you're alone? You think other people don't have these feelings?" But even Carl admits he's never been in quite the same position as me.

Mom has helped a lot, too, although I know it was really hard for her, because of my sister.

Mostly, I wish I could just stop going over it in my mind.

But it replays all the time. Like waves breaking on the narrow beach down at the river. Sometimes, after school, I walk down there to sit on the bank and do nothing. Just let the sun bake my face and listen to those waves hitting the shore, one after the other.

Tilly always follows me and I let her. Tilly's my yellow Lab. She lays down with her head on her paws and knows to leave me alone when I'm thinking. Despite everything, I still marvel at how all those tiny ripples in the water can catch the sunlight and make the river shimmer like a million jewels were strewn on the surface. Deceptive, how other times the same water can seem as smooth as glass. You'd never know that underneath, the currents run so hard and so fast.

It's a pretty river, the Corsica. But it doesn't have a heart . . .

CHAPTER TWO

In some ways, it started over a year ago. But I want to get the worst over first, so I'm going to start with what happened six months ago, in the spring. That morning, we were waiting, my two friends and I, for the ambulance to come, and J.T. took a swig from his bottle of green tea. I remember this because Digger was trying to pick a fight, and it all started with J.T.'s green tea.

No one was hurt—that's not why the ambulance was coming. My cousin Carl had this old ambulance that the county still uses for a backup, and when he had the early shift, he would swing by and give us a ride to school. School's only a couple miles away, but it's a forty-minute ride on that dang bus because we're first pickup on the loop. Besides, it was pretty cool getting a ride in the ambulance.

J.T. almost always waits for the bus with me. He lives next door on his family's chicken farm. A soybean field between my house and his has a path worn down through the middle of it we're back and forth so much. And Digger is across the road, not too far the other way. Sometimes, he walks over to join us—that, or his father will drop him off from his dump truck on his way to a job.

So we were in the driveway that morning, waiting for Carl to pick us up. Backpacks on the ground. Hunched in our parkas because it was chilly. Taking turns throwing the tennis ball for Tilly, who never quits. And Digger snatched the bottle of green tea out of J.T.'s hands and started laughing.

"What the—"

"Shhhhh!" I'm always having to tone down Digger. "My mom can hear!" And she can't stand to hear us cuss.

We cast a glance back at the house.

Digger held the bottle up, out of J.T.'s reach. "Green tea with ginseng and *honey?*" He sounded disgusted.

It made me uncomfortable, the way Digger talked to J.T. sometimes. And after all those years we spent growing up together.

But J.T. just laughed. He's pretty easygoing. And he swiped the drink back. "Hey," he said. "It's loaded with antioxidants."

"Anti *who?*" Digger screwed up his face.

"You wait, Digger," J.T. warned him. "You and Brady—especially Brady 'cause he's always out in the sun—you'll be all old and wrinkly by the time you're fifty, and I'll have, like, this perfect skin."

"Yeah, like a baby's ass," Digger retorted.

I wanted to tell him to shut up, but I didn't. I could tell when Digger was in one of his moods.

"You're just jealous," J.T. quipped.

"Of *what?*" Digger demanded.

"Guys!" I called out, stopping everything like a referee's whistle. When they looked at me, I pivoted and flung the ball for Tilly. We watched it land and roll downhill toward our dock. At the same time my father's band saw started up in the old tractor shed, which Dad has transformed into his woodworking shop. Where we live used to be a farm, but it's not anymore. The barn and the farmhouse burned down years ago—before my parents bought the property and built a one-story brick rancher. My dad is a waterman half the year, a boat carpenter the other half, and even though crabbing season started April 1, he'd been working Mondays in the shop because he was making more money building cabinets than crabbing, especially now that crabs were getting scarce.

Last year, the state legislature cut Dad's workday from fourteen hours down to eight. Then the governor took away the month of November, and it hurt us financially. My mom had to put in extra hours at the nursing home, and Dad was pretty ticked off. "They're blamin' the wrong people!" he railed. "Pollution and development—that's what's killin' us. Bay be right smart of crabs if it weren't for all the damned condo-*minions* going up!"

I don't know. We had a little argument about it after a scientist came to school. He said my dad was only half right—about the pollution and all. "We're fishing the bay too hard," that guy kept saying. "Too many crab pots, too many trotlines. You have to take the long look."

When Dad's noisy band saw stopped, I glanced at J.T. and Digger and wondered which way the conversation would go.

"What's your dad working on?" J.T. asked.

"Dr. Finney's sailboat," I said, glad to move off the subject of J.T.'s green tea. "Thirty-foot Seawind ketch. Twenty-five years old—fiberglass hull but a lot of solid wood trim topside."

J.T. arched his eyebrows. "Wow. He's got his work cut out for him."

"He's completely gutting it," I said. "Dr. Finney's going to put in this incredible electronics system. GPS. Flat-screen TV. Security." I knew this would make J.T. drool because he loves all that technical stuff.

But it only made Digger angry. He kicked a rock in the driveway. "Some people got too much money for their own damn good."

When a pair of noisy mallards flew over, we looked up. Even Tilly dropped the ball and started barking. In the west, I noticed dark clouds piling up across the horizon, like a distant mountain range.

"If the weather didn't look so bad, I'd say come on over this afternoon. We could take a little spin down the river." I felt bad for Digger sometimes. On account of his family.

"Can't go," he mumbled, still kicking his toe in the dirt. "I gotta help my old man haul gravel."

"Yeah, me neither," J.T. said. "I erased my entire hard drive last night. I need to load everything back on and rewrite that essay for English. Hey, Brady, remember those oxymorons we talked about in lit the other day?"

"Jumbo shrimp?" I asked.

"Yeah—and *military intelligence,*" J.T. reminded me.

I grinned.

"Well, I got a good one for you," J.T. said. *"Microsoft Works."*

Even Digger lifted his head and chuckled. "A *perfect idiot,"* he added.

So there we were, all of us laughing because we'd knocked out four oxymorons smack in a row—and that's when we first saw the red kayak.

From where we stood, you could see down the grassy slope behind our house, on past Dad's shop and the dock, to the creek. And out there, heading our way, was Mr. DiAngelo's new red kayak.

Digger's face lit up. "The Italian stallion," he chortled, a dual reference to the heritage of our new neighbor, Marcellus DiAngelo, and his obsession with physical fitness. Cupping his hands around his mouth, Digger pretended to call out: "Paddle hard, you sucker!"

He and J.T. exchanged this look I didn't quite catch, and J.T. started laughing, too.

But I shook my head. "He shouldn't be going out there today. When he gets down by the point—he'll *fly* down the river." I was sure Mr. DiAngelo didn't know about how the wind picked up once you left our creek and hit the open water. Not to mention the spring tides. Sometimes they were so strong they'd suck the crab-pot buoys under. I doubted whether Mr. DiAngelo knew that; he'd only had the kayak a few weeks.

"Really, guys. We ought to yell something," I said soberly.

J.T. shook his head. "He's too far away. He won't hear you."

"Why should we anyway?" Digger asked with a scowl. "Just

because you baby-sat for their little kid and you're in love with his wife?"

An overstatement if I ever heard one. Although I did take care of their son one afternoon when Mrs. DiAngelo had to go over the bridge to Annapolis for a doctor's appointment. And she is a very good-looking woman—but even J.T. and Digger thought so.

"Ben's cool," I said, trying to make light of it. "We did LEGOs."

J.T. chuckled and looked at his sneakers.

Sneering, Digger stuffed his hands in his pockets. "Look, Brady," he said, "if he's stupid enough to be out there today, he can take what's coming. Besides, he deserves it."

Tilly whined because she was waiting for me to throw the ball again.

"That water is damn cold," I said as I stooped to pick up the ball. It was only the middle of April, and the water temperature probably wasn't even fifty degrees yet. "Exposure, you know? If he fell in, he could die in, like, twenty minutes."

Digger smiled. "Exactly," he said calmly. "We'd all be so lucky."

At that point, I threw the ball so hard it landed in the marsh near the water. Tilly took off after it like a shot and disappeared into the tall grass.

"Come on." I made eye contact with Digger when I said it again: "Let's yell something."

But we didn't.

Digger dropped his eyes and backed off. When he turned in profile, I glimpsed the hard lines of his scowl as he gazed out toward that red kayak. It was the first time I realized how much anger Digger had packed inside. I knew he was sore because the DiAngelos bought his grandfather's farm, tore down the old house, and built a mansion up there on the bluff. But up until then, maybe I hadn't realized how much it bothered him.

Of course it didn't help that we'd all been booted off the property a few days ago. But if you asked me, Mr. DiAngelo was pretty nice about it. He didn't yell, or offend us, or anything like that. He merely asked us to leave because we were trespassing. And Digger *did* have that cigarette lit. I mean, Mr. DiAngelo had a right. For all he knew, we could have started a fire or something.

But from Digger's point of view, we were only hanging out under *our* cliff, where we hung out a million times over the last thirteen years. That cliff and all the property the DiAngelos now own was all part of our stomping grounds. We shot tin cans out on the cornfield. Built forts in the woods. Raced go-carts down the tractor roads. So you know, I *did* feel for some of Digger's frustration.

What I don't understand is how Digger could have been so callous that morning: *If he's stupid enough to be out there, he can take what's coming* . . . How Digger—and J.T., too—could have been so blind to the awful possibilities. Even after I reminded them: *He could die in, like, twenty minutes . . . We ought to yell something . . .*

When, exactly, did they begin to feel shamed by it?

Because it has always shamed me.

CHAPTER THREE

Carl never let us down when he arrived. He flashed the ambulance's emergency lights *and* fired a quick whirring blast from the siren as he came up our long, flat driveway. Oyster shells crunched under the weight of the ambulance, and white dust trailed behind it like smoke.

"Hey, guys!" Carl slowed the vehicle and called out his open window. "Need a lift?"

Carl's girlfriend, Mindy, dressed in her turquoise waitress uniform, was up front with him. She smiled at us.

After Mom poked her head out the side door to yell good-bye and call Tilly in, we hopped into the back of the ambulance. There was a padded bench on each side of the stretcher. We dropped our books and sat down. Then, stealthily, J.T. reached into a compartment behind him, put on a stethoscope, and secretly tried to listen to the back of Digger's head. "Nothing," he said, shaking his head. "Absolutely no brain activity."

Digger caught it from the corner of his eye and pulled

away. Then he reached up overhead and pulled off one of the elastic strips tied along the bar above the stretcher. The paramedics tie them around your arm when they need to take blood, but Digger used it like a rubber band and took aim at J.T.

I tried not to smile. "Guys, don't play with the equipment. Carl will get in trouble." Boy, how many times have I said that?

Ever since we got called on the carpet by the principal for riding in the ambulance, Carl avoided the school driveway. Instead, he dropped us off behind the 7-Eleven, next door to school.

I put the elastic strap back on the bar, then we jumped out and slammed the door.

J.T. and Digger were punching each other in the arms and made a beeline for the store, but I walked up to the front to thank Carl for the ride.

"No problem," he said. "Say, you going rock fishin' with me and your dad Saturday? Season opener."

I shrugged. "I don't know. I'm supposed to stay over J.T.'s Friday night, and Saturday's my only morning to sleep in."

"*Sleep in?*" Carl reached over and pulled the baseball cap down over my eyes. "Watermen don't sleep in!"

I turned away, embarrassed. I probably should have been getting up to pull my crab pots, but my parents didn't care if I took a morning off. I also knew Carl was kidding me. He was proud of how hard I worked. If there was more money in it, he'd be out there, too, fishing oysters and crabs year-round. He loved it. In fact, a lot of times, depending on his shift, he'd come out with me after school to haul in my catch and toss the keepers into the baskets on my skiff.

"Guess I got lazy this winter," I said, resettling the hat back on my head. It wasn't a very witty response, but I didn't feel much like joking around.

Mindy picked up on it. She was amazing that way. When she leaned forward, her long blond ponytail fell over her shoulder. "Hey, Brady," she said. "Are you okay?"

I looked from her to Carl. "I guess I am a little worried."

"About what?" Carl asked.

"Right before you came, we saw Mr. DiAngelo paddling down the creek toward the river in his red kayak."

"Your new neighbor?"

"Yeah."

Carl leaned out the window to look up at the darkening sky and rubbed a hand over his mouth. "Not a very good day," he acknowledged. "But I'm sure he knows what he's doing, Brady. He's probably already turned hisself around and gone back."

I readjusted my backpack. "You think so?" I wanted to believe that. When Carl nodded, I said, "Yeah, you're probably right." Besides, I didn't want to worry about it anymore. What I needed to think about was the algebra quiz I had first period because I hadn't studied much for it.

"Brady! Come on, we'd better get going!" J.T. called out as he came across the parking lot, stuffing a pack of caramel creams into his pocket. Digger followed with a can of Coke in his hand.

I glanced at my watch. We had five minutes before the

first bell. "Gotta run. See ya." I waved to Carl and Mindy.

Then the three of us—J.T., Digger, and I—headed across the field to Alexander Holmes Middle School.

During Spanish class, second period, I thought about the DiAngelos again. By then, I was in a better mood because the algebra quiz was easier than anyone imagined. Plus, between classes, when I was getting a drink of water at the fountain, I noticed J.T.'s sister, Katelynn, signing in late at the main office. When she waved, it made me feel kind of nice because I liked Kate. Even though she was a seventh grader, a year behind us, she was a neat kid. I pointed and grimaced, a clear reference to the cast on her leg, which was there for the ankle she broke during lacrosse practice. She made a sad face. I knew it was killing her to have to sit out the season because she loves sports.

A minute later I saw J.T. in the hall. He gave me a high five. "Act naturally," he said, but I didn't pick up on it until I was practically in the door to Spanish. When it hit me that *act naturally* was an oxymoron, I snorted. I'm sure Amy Goldberg thought I was making fun of her new braces because she was right in front of me then, but spun away, rolling her eyes. *Geez,* I thought, *I am such a klutz.*

So I saw J.T., but I never ran into Digger again that morning. It wasn't too unusual, though, because he wasn't in any of my classes except for gym.

As I said, by the time I got to Spanish, I was in a better frame of mind. Señora Mendez started off class by asking us to check one another's homework. I switched papers with

Lauren Modley, knowing I wouldn't have much work to do. Everything Lauren does is perfect. Then idly, I glanced out the window across the field, to the back of the 7-Eleven.

I couldn't hear it, but I saw a fire truck race by the store, a yellow blip, and disappear. I wondered if Carl was headed somewhere, too. A car accident, or a fire. Maybe even a hostage situation. Carl went to one last month where some guy held his wife at gunpoint in their trailer. Boy, now, that's the kind of thing I half expected Digger's dad to do someday. He's crazy and mean enough, especially when he's drinking. And he and Digger's mom have been fighting a lot.

That's when I started thinking back on the morning again. About the conversation we had in the driveway and Digger's bad mood. One thought led to another. I recalled how we got kicked off the DiAngelos' property and hoped it didn't mean Mrs. DiAngelo would never ask me to baby-sit Ben again. She paid me thirty bucks for watching him that afternoon, and she wasn't even gone four hours. That came to almost eight dollars an hour—which my dad said was a lot more than I'd make minimum wage at McDonald's.

Besides the money, though, it was neat being inside their house. Mr. DiAngelo designed it himself. Plus I got a real kick out of Ben. He's a cute kid. "A towhead," Mom called him because his hair is so blond it's almost white. He had one of those haircuts that looked like somebody put a bowl on his head and cut around it. His eyes were like two big blueberries. And when he smiled, two deep dimples appeared in the center of his cheeks.

He was only three, but you could have a decent conversation with Ben. "Bwady," he called me because he had a hard time with his *r*'s. We put together some LEGOs the afternoon I took care of him, and we constructed some fairly sophisticated stuff. A tall castle with a drawbridge that moved up and down, and a pulley with a string that hoisted soldiers up over the wall. He liked the pulley. He even used it to transport horses over the top. We made some race cars, too. Race cars for knights. Then we microwaved popcorn and watched *The Lion King* on their new DVD player. (Mrs. DiAngelo didn't want us cruising the cable.)

I promised Ben that next time I came I'd bring over my old LEGOs Aquanauts, and we'd make them dive in the bathroom sink.

"Hola! Señor Parks!" Señora Mendez shattered the daydream. *"¿Donde estas?"*

I blushed. *"Yo soy en la clase de español,"* I replied.

About a minute later, I got called down to the office.

When the classroom intercom came on, it was so loud that everyone jumped. Cassie Winfield even slapped a hand on her heart.

"Excuse me, Mrs. Mendez, could Braden Parks be dismissed immediately?" Mrs. Peters, the school secretary, had a trace of urgency to her voice. "He should come to the office with his books."

Like a bolt out of the blue.

Everyone turned to stare at me.

I held my hands palm up and looked at Señora Mendez.

"Guess you need to go," she said. "Finish Chapter Seven

for tomorrow. All of you, write this down." She peered over her reading glasses at the whole class. "Exercises one through five in the chapter review."

I had absolutely no idea why I was being dismissed. Did I have a dentist appointment I'd forgotten about? I didn't think so. As I stuffed the Spanish book into my backpack, it occurred to me I'd just seen the fire truck. Sometimes they called out the fire truck to accidents because they were afraid of fuel catching fire, or sometimes because they needed the crew to help carry someone on the backboard. My heart started beating fast. God, I hoped Mom wasn't in a wreck. Or Dad—that Dad hadn't buzzed a finger off in the workshop or something.

I swallowed hard, shoved the pen in my pocket, and hoisted my backpack.

The school hallway never seemed so long. All those lockers. All that square tile. A door closed somewhere behind me, and it was so quiet the sound echoed. I was relieved to see my father standing at the counter in the main office, talking to Mrs. Owens, our principal. But it only shifted the concern.

Mrs. Owens half smiled at me and left. Why? So we'd have privacy as he broke the news?

"Mom okay?" I asked.

Dad had his work clothes on—old jeans and a T-shirt, both flaked a little with sawdust from the shop. "Yeah, sure," he said, putting a hand on my shoulder. "Nothin' like that, Brady. Sorry if we worried you."

Relief poured out of me. I dropped the backpack on one

of the empty chairs where we sit when we're waiting in the office.

"Listen," Dad said. "Carl called. Somebody's missing on the river, maybe out in the bay. He wants us to take the boats and help look."

I put a hand over my eyes. "Oh, my God," I said.

"Brady—"

The hand slid down and I looked at my father. "It's Mr. DiAngelo, isn't it? That red kayak. We saw him this morning."

"That's what Carl said."

Dad seemed to be studying my face. "But it's not Marcellus, Brady. It's his wife. And their little boy."

CHAPTER FOUR

I was running so fast I practically slipped and fell off the dock.

"Wait!" Dad hollered. Tilly was barking at my heels, and it was hard to hear. My father rushed up behind me and handed me his cell phone. "I've got the radio on my boat."

I took the phone and pushed it into the pocket of my parka. Then both Dad and I jumped into our boats on either side of the dock.

"Go on!" I shouted at Tilly because she was tap dancing at the edge of the dock, getting ready to jump in, and I didn't want her to come.

In the pickup, on the way home from school, Dad had told me to check the smaller creeks off the river. He said he and the other rescue workers would head downstream with the currents toward the bay, the most likely course the kayak had taken. It made sense because Dad and the others had radar and searchlights on their boats. If anyone was found, Dad told me, we should go to the marina at Rock Hall, where an ambulance was waiting.

Midmorning by then, but it was dark because of the encroaching storm. Everything seemed gray: the sky, the water, the air. And all of it pressed in on me as I pulled the brim of my cap down tight and yanked the cord to start my motor. While it warmed up, I untied the lines that kept my skiff snug in its slip.

When the boat was free, I sat in the stern, pushed the gear lever to reverse, accelerated a little with a turn of my hand on the outboard's handle, and turned around backward to see where I was going. As I did, I heard a hard thump in the bow and the boat bounced forward. I swung my head back to see Tilly land awkwardly in the tiny space at the front of my skiff.

"Hey!" I yelled at her.

With precision, she hopped over the front seat and sat like an obedient soldier midboat, where there was more room. She barked once as though to tell me, *So there—now shut up.* So I did. If she wanted to go along *that* badly, there wasn't much I could do. I certainly didn't want to waste time pulling back in and forcing her out.

Switching gears to forward, I headed out, full throttle, just as fast as my skiff could go. The wind was a sheet of ice against my face and blew the dog's ears straight back. My hands were cold, too. Damn cold for April. I wished I'd brought gloves.

I was ahead of my father, but not for long. Pretty soon he had the *Miss Amanda* passing me on the right. His workboat was three times the size of my skiff, and twice as fast. He waved to me from the doghouse up front, where I could see him adjusting the radar and already picking up the radio receiver. I waved back, then Dad headed to starboard, while I veered opposite, toward the left bank of the creek.

Already my eyes were scanning the shoreline for the red kayak—or a splash of yellow. Mr. DiAngelo had told the police he couldn't remember what clothes his wife or son wore that morning, but he knew they had on yellow life jackets.

I felt excited, but a little panicked, too, as I sped down the creek, squinting into the icy spray and scanning the thick tangle of brown brush and newly budding trees along the narrow shoreline. If that red kayak was out there, I wanted to be the one to find it.

Soon I could see Dad entering the river. He was far enough ahead that I couldn't read the words *Miss Amanda* painted on his stern. I don't know what made me think of it then—maybe the panic—but I recalled the morning my sister died. The *Miss Amanda* is named for my sister. Most workboats get named for mothers or grandmothers, but my sister was the first girl born to the Parks family in two generations. And while it's true she was only an infant when she died, she was old enough to smile, and we were all nuts about her. I used to make a goo-goo face that got her so excited she wheeled her arms and legs around like a windmill.

After we lost Amanda, my mother couldn't sleep in the house and went to stay with my grandmother in Connecticut. She kept promising she would come home soon. But almost half a year went by before she did. So, for a long time, it was just Dad and me. That's the reason I spent so much time with Carl, because Dad had to work Fridays and Saturdays all winter on Mr. Fuller's oyster boat, and Mr. Fuller wouldn't allow kids on board.

Carl was training then with an ambulance crew in Annapolis, over the bridge. I even slept at the firehouse with him because he worked twenty-four-hour shifts. They were nice to me there. I liked the whole platoon. They gave me my own locker, and just like them, I taped up snapshots of my family inside the metal door. I had a picture of my rabbit and another one of my dad and mom getting hugged by a giant chocolate Kiss at Hershey Park. I had a whole pile of comic books and an old Game Boy in there, too—you know, just *stuff*—so I could be like the firefighters and the paramedics.

They never seemed to mind having a kid hanging around. I was pretty quiet, and I even helped out some, like picking up trash and emptying the ashtrays. I cooked for them, too. I learned how to cook early on because I was alone so much, and I was an expert on macaroni and cheese from the box. I'd stand up on a chair, and when the pot of water on that twelve-burner gas stove was boiling, I'd dump in eight, nine, ten boxes of macaroni at a time and stir it with a great big wooden spoon.

The rest of the time I hung out and read my comic books, or watched TV, or went out back to the pen, where I threw the ball for Jake, their bomb dog.

But sometimes, when there was room in the ambulance, Carl and the others let me ride along, in that seat behind the driver. I had to stay out of the way and be quiet, but that was easy. And that's where I learned a lot of emergency stuff.

Weird how this memory flashed through my mind as I raced the boat down the creek and into the river, my eyes sweeping back and forth across the water, looking for Ben and his mom. I saw that the ospreys were back, arranging sticks on the channel marker for their gigantic nest. And I saw some terns feeding over the sandbar. But nothing else. The motor hummed steadily, the wake behind my boat peeling away from both sides of the motor in streaks of white, green, and gray foamy water.

Not too far downstream, a small creek emptied in from the left. As my father's boat disappeared around the bend up ahead, I reluctantly turned my boat up the creek, slowed down some, and kept searching. The bow of the boat settled down, and the wake from behind sloshed up against the transom. Still nothing. Why would there be? Common sense and knowing the currents would tell you that the kayak had drifted downstream, especially with the fast-running spring tides. Unless Mrs. DiAngelo had intentionally paddled up one of the creeks, there was no way they would have *drifted* here.

God, I was cold. It started to drizzle, and the water froze on my face. I shoved my left hand under my thigh to try to keep it warm. Then I cussed out loud at myself because I hadn't called out when I saw that red kayak. I was thinking that Ben was probably freezing, too—and scared to death by now. I know what being really cold is like. Middle of winter I almost drowned in a cow pond when I was little, maybe eight. J.T., Digger, and I were playing ice hockey, and I fell clear through the ice.

The memory of that accident made me shudder. Abruptly, I leaned over to cut off the engine.

"Mrs. DiAngelo!" I hollered at the top of my lungs. "Ben! Can you hear me?"

Nothing.

"Mrs. Di-An-ge-lo!"

Not a sound. I fired up the engine again and kept going.

Up the creek, a couple private docks extended out into the water, then there was a long strip of riprap near a construction site. From that point on, it was just shoreline with trees and a lot of brown cell bush. I kept going, but toward the head of the creek, a marsh taken over by a patch of tall phragmites warned of shallow water, and I turned the boat around, not wanting to run aground. I sped up and came back down the creek, closer to the opposite bank.

Still no sign of a red kayak or a yellow life jacket. All I wanted to do was open the throttle and head downriver to where the others were searching. My hands ached they were so cold. I stuffed one hand in my pocket and hit the cell phone. I pulled it out and saw that I had "1 missed call." Turning off the motor so I could hear, I speed-dialed home to see if Mom knew anything.

"Brady—hi!" she said. "Dad called. He said they found Mrs. DiAngelo."

"They did?"

"Yes. Downriver, near Spaniard's Neck."

"Is she okay?" I asked.

"She's alive," Mom said. "But just barely. They have *not* found Ben."

"They didn't?"

"No. They lost the kayak, Brady. So Ben is out there some-where in the water in his life jacket."

"Oh, man, it's *cold,* Mom—"

"I know. . . I know it's cold. Are you all right? Can you do this, Brady?"

"I'm all right. I'm fine," I assured her. "I need to keep looking!"

I ended the call and put the phone back in my pocket. We had to move really fast now. If Ben was in the water, his time was limited.

Tilly started barking as I picked up speed.

"Quiet!" I hollered.

I wondered if I should waste my time going up any of these little creeks and inlets now that they had found Mrs. DiAngelo downriver. But Tilly was barking up a storm and stood with her nose pointed toward the riverbank, where some of the water curled into a small cove.

It was hard to ignore Tilly's instincts. Once, she barked at the ceiling in our basement so insistently that my father pulled down part of the insulation and found a possum's nest made out of leaves.

"Better not be a squirrel or something stupid like that," I

grumbled as I swung the boat toward the cove. I bit my lip uncertainly.

Suddenly Tilly had her front paws up on the edge of my boat. Her tail thumped back and forth, hitting my knees.

"What is it, Til?" I asked, squinting to see through the drizzle.

I slowed down the motor as we approached the narrow channel to the cove. Tall marsh grass obscured my view to the right, but as soon as we had motored around it, I glimpsed the remains of an old dock—a place where J.T., Digger, and I used to fish—and a single, bright spot of yellow.

CHAPTER FIVE

It was Ben. But as I drew closer I could see that he was motionless, his small body hunched forward, the back of his life jacket caught on a jagged piece of old piling that jutted out of the water like a rotten tooth.

"Ben! Are you okay?" I hollered, pulling the boat up alongside.

His eyes weren't right.

"Move!" I ordered Tilly. Right away she jumped back into the narrow space in the bow.

I flipped the engine into neutral and reached over to pull in Ben. He was a lot heavier than I would have thought, probably because he was so waterlogged. The water was cold, too. I grabbed hold of the collar on his life jacket and summoned all my strength to "unhook" him from that piece of wood. For a second, I lost my balance and nearly went in headfirst myself. But I fell backward instead, never letting go, and managed to pull Ben into my boat on top of me. It was a rough landing, and I hit my elbow hard on the gunnel. I just hoped I hadn't hurt Ben.

The first thing I did was get his wet life jacket off—that and his soaked parka. Then I took off my own coat, wrapped it around him, and put my baseball cap on his head. I rubbed his hands. I patted his cheeks. But he looked terrible lying there on the damp wooden floor of my boat, his face pale as a sheet, his eyes half shut and his lips as blue as a fresh bruise.

I was scared to death because I didn't know what to do! I pulled the cell phone out of my pocket, but my hand was shaking so bad that the phone slipped right out of my grasp, hit the edge of the boat, and disappeared into the water.

"Oh, no!" I exclaimed.

I looked back at Ben. He needed help. I had to quit messing around.

What do I do? What do I do? I was asking myself. *What would Carl do?* And I remembered those guys at the fire station talking about the ABC's. The first thing you did in an emergency was ABC's.

A was airways. I looked at Ben's nose. Clear as far as I could tell. Quickly, but gently—I knew you had to handle cold people carefully because of their hearts, their hearts can go kind of nuts and not beat right—I rolled him onto his left side. Some water trickled out of his mouth.

"Good," I said out loud. "Good, Ben."

B was what? *B* was breathing. Was Ben breathing?

I pulled the choke out to flood the motor and shut it off

so I could hear. But I couldn't hear anything! I put a finger under his nose and didn't feel anything. Was it because my fingers were numb with cold? I stared at his chest, but I couldn't see it moving. Quickly, I felt with two fingers against his throat for that artery, the big one up there under your jaw. But I couldn't feel anything.

No, I decided. Ben wasn't breathing.

Quickly now—I knew I had to—I rolled Ben back onto his back, then I bent over, pinched his nose shut, covered his small mouth with mine, and gave him two breaths. His lips were so cold they didn't feel real.

I checked again. He still wasn't breathing.

C. I remembered that *C* was circulation. Ben needed his blood to be moving around, too.

"Oh, God," I moaned, thinking: *I've got to do it. I've got to do CPR!* I had been taught how—Dad and I took a class at the community center. We practiced on a dummy, and I watched Carl do it more than once. But would I remember?

I tilted Ben's head back a little, pinched his nose again, and started by giving him one breath. Then I sat up, put the heel of my right hand on his chest, covered it with my left, and pressed down. Five times I pressed down. Five compressions. Then I bent over for another breath. Then five compressions. Then another breath. Then five compressions.

I did not think about anything else as I did this. All I was doing was counting and pushing and breathing and praying inside that Ben would start breathing.

"Come on, Ben!" I begged him.

Five compressions. Then another breath. *Breathe, Ben, breathe!*

Ben needed to get to that ambulance fast. I had to get him down to the marina at Rock Hall. It wasn't that far, but I wasn't going to get there sitting here in the creek.

Five compressions. Another breath.

I paused long enough to start the motor again and put the boat in gear.

Five compressions. One breath.

Then I headed my skiff in the right direction, grabbed the stern line, and looped it around the outboard's handle.

Back to Ben. Five compressions. One breath.

Quickly, I reached for the stern line and wrapped it around a cleat to keep the motor straight.

Five compressions. Another breath.

As if all that wasn't bad enough, it started to rain hard, too.

I ignored it. I ignored the rain, the cold—everything—and just continued. Five compressions, another breath, a quick check to make sure the boat was headed in the right direction.

I glanced up and down, but there was no one in the river. No one! I headed the boat downstream to Rock Hall and kept working on Ben.

Five compressions, one breath. All the way down the river with the rain lashing my face and blurring my eyes until I saw a whirring ambulance light at the landing in the distance.

I kept on with the CPR. I knew I couldn't stop. Maybe I should have. I could have slammed the boat into high gear and opened the throttle. But I also knew that Ben needed me to keep breathing into him.

Five compressions, one breath. We were almost at the landing. I heard someone yell my name, and Tilly started barking. Then more people were hollering, and there was a bank of flashing lights. At least two police cars, an ambulance. It was all a welcome blur. I continued with five compressions, one breath.

Suddenly Jimmy Landers, one of Carl's coworkers, was hollering real loud. "Keep it up, Brady! Keep it up! That's it! Pull the boat in—we've got it! Don't stop, Brady!"

Things happened even faster after that. Jimmy was down beside me taking over, then lifting Ben up onto the dock, where Carl took him and continued the CPR. Then Jimmy jumped back up on the dock, too, and I saw Carl place his fingers on Ben's neck, checking for a pulse. Someone else pulled in the boat while Carl and Jimmy kept working on Ben, even as they carried him to the ambulance.

Before a policeman closed the back doors of the ambulance, Carl shouted, "We've got a pulse!" There wasn't time for him to say anything more. The doors were closed and the ambulance took off, siren wailing, lights flashing.

Completely out of breath, I stood on the landing—I don't have a clue how I got there—and watched the lights disappear. I thought about how we were all going to be on that rescue show. We were all going to be on *Rescue 911*, I thought. All of us, I bet. Tilly, too.

A policeman came over and put his arm around my shoulders. "Good job, son," he said. He led me over to his cruiser and gave me a jacket. "Go ahead. Get inside and warm up."

"My dog," I mumbled. I was so out of breath I felt dizzy. "I can't leave my dog in the boat."

The policeman called for someone to get Tilly, and both of us, Tilly and I, got in the backseat of the cruiser to warm up.

"They're taking him over to Lester Krebb's field, where they've got a medevac helicopter coming," the policeman told me. He pulled out a notebook. "When you're ready, I need you to give us a little report."

I told him how I had found Ben. When the officer was satisfied, he offered me a ride home in the cruiser. But I wanted to get my boat back, too. I assured him I could get home on my own.

"I don't doubt it," he said, grinning.

The rain had let up some, so the policeman let us go. He said he would call both my parents to let them know I was okay and that I was headed home.

Back in the boat, I put Ben's life jacket and his soaked parka to one side and picked up my Orioles hat from the floor, where I'd done the CPR on Ben. It must have fallen off when they picked him up. It felt a little strange, putting that hat back on my head after what it had just been through. But my head was cold. And I needed to get started.

Everyone else had left the landing by then. It was over. I began to feel a little relieved. Tilly and I headed upriver just as it started to rain hard again. But Carl's voice—*We've got a pulse!*—echoed in my ears, and I smiled. I think I could have driven through a blizzard right then. I felt both drained and elated.

I'll tell you this: I am not the type of person who prays very much. Hardly at all really. But about a minute later, I stopped that boat right in the middle of the Corsica River, in the pouring rain, to fold my hands. I just sat there with the engine in neutral, resting my head against the fingers of my tightly folded hands, because it had just hit me what happened. I'm not saying I cried, mind you, but I did have tears in my eyes.

I thought about how it all happened. About fate. I mean, what if Dad hadn't been working in the shop that Monday? Normally, he'd be out on the water. If he had been, he wouldn't have come to get me out of school. There wouldn't have been the extra person to check the little creeks and coves the way I did.

I knew then I would never be the same person anymore. Because that day on the Corsica River, the day I lifted Ben off the piling, I had straddled the invisible line between life and death that runs down all our lives every second—with every breath we take. And thanks to some good luck and timing—thanks to Tilly, and God, too—I had pulled Benjamin DiAngelo from one side to the other.

CHAPTER SIX

I didn't set out to be a hero. Honest. I just wanted Ben and his mother to be okay.

It's true I thought about that rescue show. I even wondered if they'd ask Tilly and me to do the reenactment. And I was sure Mrs. DiAngelo would thank me personally because she was such a nice person. I even envisioned her bringing me a plate of that almond biscotti I raved about at her house. But I didn't think anyone else would make a real big deal out of what happened.

As I drove the boat home after the rescue, I made a decision. I would give Ben my entire set of LEGOs Aquanauts. The little deep-sea divers had been my favorites. But I didn't play with them anymore, and I kind of liked the idea of Ben having them there when he got home from the hospital.

At the dock, Mom waited for me under an umbrella. I wondered how much the policeman had told her when he called. I also wondered what she and Dad were going to say when they found out I dropped our cell phone in the water.

Slowing the motor, I steered my skiff up close to shore so Tilly could hop out in the shallow water. Then I backed the boat up into the slip, turned off the motor, wrapped lines from the dock around my cleats, and threw Ben's coat and life jacket up on the dock. The wooden ladder was slick from the rain. I held tight as I took each step and pulled myself up onto the dock.

"I just talked to Carl," Mom said, opening her arms.

I hugged her back. Tilly ran up on the dock and nuzzled our legs, her big, wet body practically knocking us over. I was glad to be home, but my heart still pounded. And every time I thought of how Ben looked with his eyes half closed and his lips all blue, I turned to jelly inside.

"Come and get some dry clothes on," my mother said, pushing the wet hair off my forehead. When she bent over to pick up Ben's stuff, I offered to carry it.

Tilly shook herself off and walked up the hill with us.

It had only been a few hours since I left for school that morning, but as I entered the house, it felt as though I'd been away for a year. The smallest things seemed so welcoming. The vase Mom had made in her pottery class filled with dried cattails. The small mahogany table with the picture of me from sixth grade. The way Dad's dirt-caked work boots rested on a piece of newspaper inside the door.

I put Ben's things on the floor and wiped Tilly off with an old bath towel we kept in a basket inside the front door. Then I took off my wet shoes and went down the hall to my room. When I opened the door, a bubbling, underwater sound filled my ears. It was only the fish-tank screensaver

I'd left on the computer, but I turned it off before taking a long, hot shower. By the time I was getting dressed again, I could hear my father's voice in the kitchen.

Mom had a cup of hot chocolate waiting for me and pulled out a chair.

"Good job, Brady," Dad said, shaking my hand, then pulling me over for a big hug. He was wet to the bone, but I didn't care. "Some morning, wasn't it?"

"Unbelievable," I said. "Where were *you?*"

"Most of us went on down the river toward Queenstown thinkin' the current pulled the kayak that way. We figured they'd all end up in the bay, probably down toward the bridge somewhere."

"You know, it was Tilly who made me look over toward that little place off the river," I told Dad. "I'm not sure I would have gone in there and seen Ben if Tilly hadn't barked up a storm."

"Good girl!" Dad clapped his hands softly, and Tilly rushed to him for a vigorous scratch behind the ears.

"I forgot about that place," I told Dad. "You know where I'm talking about? J.T., Digger, and I used to go fishing there? Swimming, too, sometimes."

"Oh, yeah. There's an old dock—"

"That's it!" I said.

"Well, I'll be." Dad shook his head and patted my shoulder. Then he went to change into dry clothes. Afterward, we sat at the kitchen table for a long time talking about everything, so Mom heard the whole story a couple of times. She made us thick turkey sandwiches, then cut up an apple and sliced some cheese. Both Dad and I were starved for lunch.

It felt great to have done what I did and to have both my parents so proud of me. They didn't even care about the cell phone I lost. Dad dismissed it with a wave of his hand. "We can get another one of those easy."

Before we even finished eating, though, the telephone started ringing. Word had gotten around. The first call was from Carl, who had just driven the ambulance back to the station. My father talked to him briefly, then handed me the phone.

"You okay?" Carl asked.

"Fine," I said. "How's Ben?"

"They airlifted him over to Children's Hospital down in D.C.," Carl said.

"Did his mother go, too?"

"No, but his father was there. He went," Carl said. "They took the mother down to Easton. But I think she's okay, Brady. She was able to talk a little after they got her warmed up at the hospital."

"Did she tell you what happened?" I still didn't know how they lost the kayak.

"She says it was getting windy and rough. She tried to take it to shore, some little cove somewhere, she said. She was almost to shore, but couldn't quite make it because the kayak was so full of water. All of a sudden, she said, it was gone. She said she managed to hook Ben to a piece of old piling before she got pulled out with the current."

"How long were they in the water?" I asked.

"She's not sure."

"Did she say *why,* Carl? *Why'd* they go out there on such a bad day?"

"Ben wanted a ride before they went away for a couple days. She said he loved that kayak and begged for one little ride before they left."

While he was talking, I tried to picture in my mind what had happened and felt all over again how scared they must have been.

"I just wanted to tell you what a super job you did, Brady. Everyone's talking about it. Down here at the station, we're real proud of you. I told your dad, I said, 'Let the kid take tomorrow off, he deserves it.'"

"Oh—thanks, Carl. But I can't. I've got a social studies exam."

"Suit yourself," Carl said. "You want a ride in the morning? I'll flash my lights for you all the way."

"Nah, it's okay." I knew tomorrow was Carl's day off. "I can take the bus."

"All right. But you take it easy, you hear?"

"I will."

We hung up, and right away the phone rang again. This time it was Captain Dressler from the fire department telling me what a superb effort I had made. He said he was going to recommend me for some kind of award.

Later, after school was out, the phone rang some more. Two kids from my class wanted to know if it was true. My uncle Henry down in Grasonville called to say he heard about it at the gas station. Then, at eight o'clock that night, when I was taking Tilly outside, a reporter called.

I had talked to a reporter once before, when I was nine and a newspaper did a story on me being one of the youngest kids in Maryland to have a commercial crab license. It was different then because Mom and Dad were with me, and they did half the talking. This time Mom asked me first if I wanted to be interviewed. When I shrugged, she handed me the phone and went back to the kitchen.

"Here," Dad offered. "I'll take Tilly outside."

I sat down in Dad's chair in the living room and put my feet up on the hassock while the reporter and I talked. He seemed like a nice guy. Craig somebody. He said what I did was pretty amazing, and he wanted to hear the whole story—everything. So I told him. Except that I didn't include how we'd seen the red kayak that morning, and how we didn't bother to call out a warning.

"Were you scared?" Craig asked me.

"Of what?"

"Of getting lost out there yourself? Or maybe not finding him in time?"

I sort of snorted. "I wasn't afraid of getting lost 'cause I know the river pretty well. But I *was* worried that if they were in the water, the cold would get to them before any of us could."

"They tell me you knew the kid. What's his name? Ben?" I could hear him tapping on his computer. "You took care of Ben a couple times?"

"I baby-sat for him once," I said.

"So you're pretty relieved he survived."

"*Very* relieved," I assured him.

"Are you worried about what might happen to him yet?"

"What do you mean?" I asked.

Craig somebody paused. "You know, are you worried that Ben was in the cold water so long he'll have some kind of permanent brain damage or something?"

Man. I had not even thought of that!

"Brady? . . . Brady, you there?"

"Yeah, I'm here," I sort of mumbled into the phone. "Sure I'm worried."

We wrapped it up then. I told him I needed to go. Craig somebody said that the story would likely lead the state page in the morning, but I told him we didn't get the Baltimore paper.

When we were finished, I hung up and told my mother that I just wanted to study for tomorrow's exam and get to bed early. I also had some Spanish homework. No way was Señora Mendez going to let me off the hook just because I rescued someone.

But the truth was, I didn't want to take any more calls. I was talked out. Plus, I couldn't stand the thought that Ben might end up with some kind of brain damage.

I took a grocery bag and went to my room, where I closed the door. First thing I did was pull the plastic box out from my closet and noisily paw through all the LEGOs, picking out the red and black Aquanauts with the little oxygen tanks on their backs. Then I scooped up two of the sharks. A white one and a gray one. Ben would like the sharks, I thought, the way they could open and close their jaws.

I put the bag on my desk and sat on the edge of my bed, thinking.

At the nursing home, where my mother worked, one of the patients had a grandson named Andy who had brain damage. Andy, in his wheelchair, came to visit a lot because he didn't have much else to do. Sometimes, they left Andy there all day to sit in the common room, where the residents played bingo or cards. The residents didn't mind. If I happened to walk in, to see Mom or something, I always went over to Andy and said, "Hi, how's it going?" I know he can hear, because he moves his head, but he can't quite focus, or work his hands the right way to wave.

Man, I just couldn't stand to see Ben like that. All twisted in a wheelchair. I reached over for a pillow, doubled it up, and hit it hard with my fist. I'd rather be dead, I thought, than brain damaged.

CHAPTER SEVEN

In the morning, it was nonstop from the minute Dad came back from the 7-Eleven with three copies of the Baltimore paper. He spread out the Maryland page on the table so we could see the headline and the story:

BOY RESCUES TODDLER FROM RIVER

A thirteen-year-old Eastern Shore boy, alone in his 14-foot skiff, plucked a three-year-old from the frigid waters of the Corsica River yesterday afternoon and resuscitated the child while speeding through pelting rain to waiting rescuers.

Braden "Brady" Parks was one of a dozen people, including fire and rescue, law enforcement officials, and watermen, who responded to an emergency call yesterday morning that Virginia DiAngelo, 30, and her young son, Benjamin, were missing on the river.

Virginia DiAngelo is reported in good condition this

45

morning at Easton General Hospital, while Benjamin, who was flown to the pediatric intensive care unit at Children's Hospital, remains in critical condition. Both suffered from prolonged exposure in waters estimated at 48 degrees yesterday when their kayak overturned.

Thomas Parks, a waterman who aided the rescue effort, summoned his son, Brady, from school. "I figured Brady knew those waters as well as anybody," Mr. Parks said.

But the younger Parks insisted he could not have done it alone. "Part of the credit goes to my dog, Tilly," said Brady, an eighth grader at Alexander Holmes Middle School. "She pointed me in the right direction."

So on and so forth. The whole story.

On the bus, the driver saluted me. And at school, all kinds of people patted me on the shoulder, shook my hand, or gave me a thumbs-up.

While I was at my locker, Mrs. Owens, the principal, came over and put her arm around my shoulders. "Good for *you*," she said into my ear, embarrassing the heck out of me because I was surrounded by kids who overheard everything she said. "I received a call from Channel Thirteen in Baltimore. They want to come out this afternoon and do an interview."

"Is it okay with my parents?" I asked.

"It's fine with them. Do you want to do it?"

I had never been on television before. Lauren Modley hugged her books and stared at me, her eyes doubling in size.

"Sure," I said, shrugging.

Not too long afterward, eighth grade had an assembly in the gym to talk about the upcoming orientation day we were going to have over at the county high school. And at the end of it, Mrs. Owens announced: "If you haven't already heard, we have a bona fide hero in our midst this morning. Brady Parks." Everyone in my class stood up and clapped. I know I blushed from head to toe, but man, what I wouldn't give to experience that moment again.

It was terrific how everyone at school responded. Everyone except for J.T. and Digger, that is—my *best friends*. They didn't come over to wait for the bus with me that morning. And although I spotted them at the assembly, they didn't save me a seat or anything, so I didn't get to talk to them. And I never knew what they were thinking. Were they sorry we hadn't called out to Mrs. DiAngelo? Embarrassed because they had cheered on a near tragedy? What? What were they thinking?

It started to hurt my feelings that they never sought me out. But I wasn't going to let on that I was miffed. I even had an oxymoron ready for J.T. When I saw him, and he commented on the rescue, I was going to say, "Yeah, it was *pretty ugly.*"

The other thing was this: Almost the whole time in school, I didn't let myself think anything bad was going to happen to Ben. I was a little swept up in being a hero, I guess. I'd never been one before, and it felt pretty neat. Plus, I was sure that if something *was* wrong with Ben, the doctors at the hospital would have known it by then. Someone would have told me.

Still, every once in a while I couldn't help but think about that reporter's question, and a sick feeling churned my stomach. I was eager to tell J.T. about it. I decided I'd say something to him when we were together in social studies class right after lunch. Before we took the exam. But by then, everything had flipped upside down and I was gone. Taken out of school, *fast,* by my mother.

CHAPTER EIGHT

Brady, I need to talk to you." Mom's voice, so close, startled me.

I whirled around from my locker. "What in the world—"

"Please Brady," she said firmly, grabbing my forearm. "Outside. I need to talk to you."

I was a little stunned. It wasn't like either of my parents to just show up in school the way they had the last two days.

But I didn't argue. Mom was harried; in fact, her hair wasn't totally dry, and I realized that she was wearing the purple sweater she only wears to work, but with a pair of jeans, like she was half dressed.

Pushing our way through all the kids and commotion, I followed her to the front entrance. I thought sure someone would make a wisecrack. But no one seemed to notice my mother. If they did, they didn't care. "Way to go, Brady!" one boy down the hall yelled.

When the heavy front doors closed behind us, we looked at each other. It was cold, and neither one of us had a jacket.

"What is it?" I asked.

She hesitated and started rubbing her arms to get warm, but then she decided she wasn't going to tell me there, on the front steps of the school, either.

"Let's get in the car for a minute," she said, heading off toward our Jeep, which was parked at the curb.

It was getting weird.

We got into the front seats, and when my mother pulled her door closed and sighed, it hit me. She had bad news about Ben. Ben was in a coma or something. He *did* have brain damage. Somehow, they already knew that he would never be the same.

Instead, Mom turned to me and said, "Ben died."

At first, I didn't think I heard right.

"What? What did you say?"

"Ben is dead, Brady. He died this morning. It was on the news. I thought I'd better get to school before someone told you in the hallway, or those television people showed up."

"But he was alive," I tried to argue. "Carl had a pulse!"

"I know." She looked down at the steering wheel and nodded.

The news threw me off. Slowly, I fell back in the seat and stared straight out the windshield. As I did, the Cloverland Dairy milk truck pulled away from where it was backed up to the school for delivery. When it passed in front of us, the smiling, black-and-white cow painted on its side was unavoidable. And in that instant I thought to myself, *Ben is never going to drink any more milk.* Stupid. But that was my first thought: Ben would never drink another cup of milk from those little spout cups of his.

I felt my mother's hand touch mine. "I am so sorry, Brady," she said. "I know this is going to be hard for you."

"Why?" I demanded, turning to her. "Why did he die?"

Mom's eyes shone. I could see she'd been crying and figured this hurt her, too, because it was a little like when we lost Amanda.

"I don't know," she replied. When she blinked, a tear ran down her cheek. "I guess because he was in that cold water for so long."

I felt my own eyes fill up. "Shoot!" I exclaimed, kicking at a Kleenex box on the floor. "I should have gotten there faster!"

"No, Brady!" Mom tried to grab my hand, but I pulled it away and put it up over my face.

"It's not your fault. Don't you dare blame yourself. You *tried,* Brady. You did everything you could. If you hadn't found him and done what you did, he wouldn't have had any chance. You *at least* gave him that!"

Did I? Did I do everything I could?

An enormous hole opened in my chest. I took in a huge gulp of air and held it for a moment. Then I grew still.

When I took my hand away from my eyes, I saw the dairy truck disappear down the highway and watched the noisy sixth graders run out onto the field for gym.

If we talked anymore, I can't remember. All I know is Mom said, "Let's go home." And we did.

———

For a while I sat at the kitchen table, numb, while Mom called school and made sure the television interview had been canceled. Then I moved into my room and sat at the end of my bed, staring at the floor. I started thinking that the only thing I wanted to do was go find that red kayak and bring it in. It seemed like a small, insignificant thing. The DiAngelos probably would never want to see it again. But it's all I could think of doing.

So I changed into grubby jeans and reached for my hat, my Baltimore Orioles cap, but then I thought, no, this was the hat that Ben wore just before he died. Not that I'm superstitious, but I didn't feel right about it. I set it down on my bureau and took another instead, then grabbed one of Dad's winter coats because now both of mine were gone— one in the ambulance with Ben and the other one at school—and headed down to the dock.

Tilly followed at my heels. She wanted to come in the worst way, but I wouldn't let her in the boat. I don't know why. "Go on!" I hollered at her when she barked and tried to hop in after I undid the lines.

I motored straight to the spot in the cove where I had found Ben, cut off the engine, and let the boat drift.

I was trying real hard not to think of how I messed up. How I could have called out a warning when we first saw them. But even if I had yelled, would Mrs. DiAngelo have heard me? And if she had, would she have *listened*? Who knows? I should have tried, though. At least then she would have been alerted to the danger—and maybe she would have come back before it was too late. Or maybe I could have found Ben earlier. Just think—if I hadn't gone up that other creek first. If I'd gotten there *five minutes sooner* . . .

The fact that I went from being a hero to a great big nothing in just a few hours didn't bother me. The other stuff was too big.

The water was calm, solid brown because of how the rain had stirred everything up the day before. You could still smell the storm, the wet logs, the damp grass, the muddy riverbank. I knew I'd never find the kayak. Most likely it had gone out with the tide and floated downriver. Either that or it was washed up somewhere along the bay's shore, maybe even as far south as the bay bridge. A kayak was pretty hard to sink. It would turn up eventually. But what would it matter? What was I going to do with it anyway?

Usually, being out on the water made me feel free. Whenever things at school bothered me, I went out on the water to shake it off. But that day all it did was make me sick to my stomach. I noticed how, nearby, the roots to a big sweet gum tree, exposed by erosion in the riverbank, suddenly looked like a swarm of snakes slithering into the water.

Just then, the eagle flew over and split the air in half with his terrible screech. Made me jump it was so loud. You hardly ever saw the eagle—a pair of them lived nearby—let alone heard one. But I figured it was yelling at me. It saw everything that happened in the river yesterday and it was letting me know.

Unfair, I thought. My teeth clenched and a tremendous surge of anger burst out of me. "You didn't have to kill him!" I screamed at the river.

My voice echoed in the hollow that surrounded the quiet cove. *Kill him, kill him, kill him . . .* "You didn't have to be so cold," I accused, but the anger was gone, turned into something else already. "You didn't have to make Ben die," I muttered before I began to cry.

Some people, I guess, they'd be railing at God for letting a thing like that happen. But me, I cussed out the river. And you know what? Nothing happened. When I finished crying, there wasn't a sound to be heard except for the gentlest lap of waves on the nearby sandbar. The river didn't care.

A strange, chilly feeling settled around me then, like an invisible fog. What was I going to do? And whatever compelled me to look down I'll never know. But this is the truth: When I leaned over to peer into the river, the water was not brown and full of sediment, but perfectly clear. And at the bottom, a few feet down, I could see the red kayak.

CHAPTER NINE

It freaked me out seeing that kayak under the water. At home, I hid in my room and didn't tell either of my parents about it. I halfway thought I was going nuts, and that kind of thinking scared me a little.

Mom brought me some dinner, a grilled cheese and some soup, but it sat there growing cold until I gave the sandwich to Tilly. Dad came in later. He was worn out from crabbing all day.

I was at my desk and pushed my chair back, glad that Dad had come in.

"Good run," he reported. "Hauled in fifteen bushels. Mostly females, though," he said, disappointed. Females didn't bring in half the value of a good-size jimmy.

I hoped Dad would sit on the end of my bed and stay because I wanted to tell him how twisted up I felt inside.

"Glad you ate the sandwich," he said.

I glanced at Tilly.

"Your mother was gettin' worried. You know how she is."

"I'm okay," I said too quickly. "I think I am anyway. I'm not sure."

My father pushed his hands into his pockets. "Look, Brady," he said. "Don't be blamin' yourself. You were a hero yesterday for all you done. Finding Ben and givin' him CPR and gettin' him on down to Rock Hall. We're proud of what you done. The way it turned out—" He shook his head. "It's not your fault. I just don't want you to be blamin' yourself, son."

I nodded. I appreciated everything he said, but he didn't know how bad I felt about not calling out a warning when I'd seen the kayak that morning, before school.

"You can stay home tomorrow, if you want."

"Thanks," I said. But a day off from school was not what I needed. I wanted to tell Dad about how scared I was, how I *still* felt responsible. The words stuck in my throat, though.

Dad sighed. "Why don't you turn in? Get you some sleep."

I knew Dad hated to talk about feelings and stuff like that. It's one reason my mother left for such a long time after Amanda died. Leastways that's what I heard her tell Grandma once on the telephone. *You know Tom, I can't tell him how I feel about anything . . .*

"Well, I'm gonna hit the tick," Dad said, turning to go. "Got to get up early and make a run 'fore that nor'easter comes in. More rain, they're sayin'."

I nodded. I knew I'd lost my chance to talk.

Softly, Dad closed the door.

After he left, I sat, staring at the Michael Jordan poster

on the back of my bedroom door. J.T. and Digger had the same poster because we played basketball a lot. I gave them the poster when Jordan made his comeback with the Washington Wizards.

I turned around then and powered up the computer to see if there was any e-mail for me and saw that I had two messages. One from Lauren Modley, saying she was really sorry for what had happened to the little boy, and what a brave thing I had done. The other from J.T. It wasn't much. Just this: *Brady: Sorry for what happened.*

At least he had acknowledged it, I thought.

That night, I couldn't sleep.

For hours, I lay in my bed thinking about the DiAngelos and wondering what they were doing. I knew that Mrs. DiAngelo was in the hospital, but where was Mr. DiAngelo? Was he at the hospital, too? Or was he home alone, watching TV? Or sitting on his back steps crying? And what about Ben? Did they cover him up with a sheet the way you see in the movies? Was he in a room alone? Where? Was his spirit up in heaven already? And what was *that* like? Would he—or his parents—ever know how hard I tried?

I got up twice to get a drink of water. I got up just to look out the window. And I got up once to take Tilly outside and stood for a long time in my mother's butterfly garden outside the back kitchen door. It was clear and cold, with just enough moonlight to see the little brick path Dad had made. All the different bushes, so pretty in summer, were brown and broken from the long winter. But there was a measure of comfort standing in the butterfly garden because I knew it was there for Amanda.

The sweet, painful memory of my sister had paled over the years, but I would never forget. I was seven years old when she came and went—and we never *ever* talked about Amanda. We don't even refer to her—leastways not in front of my mother. There is nothing in our house to even suggest Amanda ever existed. Not a stuffed animal, or a picture, or a piece of her clothing—nothing. My parents packed some stuff in a trunk and got rid of the rest. Then they locked that trunk and put it in a corner of the attic. The only thing left was Amanda's name on the back of Dad's boat, and Dad wasn't about to paint over it. Despite my mother, he stood his ground on that one.

I scuffed down the brick path a ways and thought about how some things had changed forever that morning my parents found Amanda in her crib, not breathing. My mother blamed herself—she kept crying about how she should have checked on the baby during the night. And I wondered if Mrs. DiAngelo would blame herself the same way. Would she regret not telling Ben it was too cold to go out in the kayak? Or that they didn't have time? Or that she couldn't find the life jackets?

God, I thought, *why didn't I just yell something?*

In my weaker moments, I still think she might have heard me.

Back inside, I tried to sleep again, but I couldn't even close my eyes.

At 4 A.M., when I heard Dad get up to go crabbing, I got up to go with him. Maybe out there, we'd find time to talk, I thought. Maybe that would help. I wasn't sure. I only knew that I couldn't sleep and I didn't want to be in bed, alone in the dark, anymore.

"You're up?" Dad rubbed his eyes. He was surprised, but he is not one to make a big deal out of anything.

"I want to go with you."

He didn't blink an eye. "All right by me," he said. "Why don't you fix us some sandwiches while I get dressed."

I was glad for the work. I put together four thick sandwiches with cold cuts, American cheese, and lots of mustard and mayonnaise. Put them in little plastic bags and threw them in a cooler with some blue ice and a couple of apples and bananas. I tossed in a box of Oreos, too, then a big bottle of grapefruit juice for Dad and two cans of Dr Pepper for me.

By the time I was finished making lunch and got myself dressed, Dad had fixed his thermos of coffee and was ready to go, too. We headed out together, Tilly left to whimper inside the back door. Because it was still dark, we had to use a flashlight to see our way down to the toolshed, where my father kept his bait in two old refrigerators. We pulled out five bushels of brown razor clams, dumped them in our baskets, and carried them down to the workboat. It took us two trips to get all the bait on board.

While Dad checked everything on the *Miss Amanda*—the water, the oil, the fuel—I turned on the radar, flipped the lights on and off, and turned both the VHF and the AM/FM radio on. Dad liked a country music station out of Baltimore, which drove me nuts, but I left it on low, figuring I'd better not say anything since I was missing a day of school to be there.

By five-thirty, we were ready to set out. Dad liked working his first hour or so in the dark because he could beat the wind that way. The wind comes up between eight and ten in the morning, and if it's in your face, it makes the job more time-consuming. "You gotta beat the wind to make time," Dad always says. "And you gotta make time."

Outside in the brisk air, with a few early songbirds starting up and our eyes getting used to the darkness, I felt a little bit better, like somehow life was going on.

After we cast off the lines, Dad let me go up front to the doghouse to drive the workboat out of its slip into the creek. Then he came in a few seconds later, to pick up the radio and check in with his best waterman friend, Kenny O'Leary. Kenny kept his boat up near Rock Hall with most of the local crabbers, and was just stocking his boat, so Dad said, "See you out there" as we left the creek and turned into the river. If you kept going south, on down past Queenstown, the river would hook around in the west, then the north and empty into the Chesapeake Bay, but mostly we crabbed the river.

We didn't talk about Ben or what had happened. We stepped into our rubber overalls, pulled on our rubber gloves, and started winching in crab pots, dumping out crabs, and refilling the bait holders with clams. I figured that eventually the subject would come up.

About an hour later, there was a beautiful sunrise.

"Lookee there," Dad said, pausing to wipe sweat off his forehead with the back of his hand. We paused a moment to marvel at how the rising rim of gold sun silently announced itself by illuminating the sky with brilliant, broad streaks of pink, purple, and orange.

"Just think," Dad went on as he plucked out a small crab from the wooden bin where everything from each pot got dumped and sorted. "You and me, Brady, we seen more sunrises in a month than some people see their whole lives." He tossed the undersize crab back in the water.

It was true. A good sunrise was awesome. I watched the little crab dart away beneath the waves. His second chance, I thought. Maybe he'd live and grow big enough to become a keeper one day.

At 10 A.M. we sat on top of the huge engine box in the middle of the boat and had lunch. By then I was pretty hungry, but after half a sandwich, I didn't feel like eating anymore.

Dad noticed. "You can change the station if you want."

"That's okay," I told him. I wished he had asked how I was feeling instead. "It's not the station," I said, but he didn't bite.

Still, being out there with Dad, seeing that beautiful sky—it should have done more for me.

By late morning, we had several bushels of crabs sitting there, all separated in bushel baskets. There was a short row, four bushels of number-one males—those five and three-quarters inches or more. Then three baskets of mixed males, five to five and three-quarters. And four bushel baskets of females.

"Was a time when I'd have twice as many crabs here for the work we done this mornin'," Dad said soberly as he surveyed the catch.

"But the price is up," I said, shrugging. "We caught less, but we made more per bushel, didn't we?"

My father lifted his cap and scratched the back of his head. "Ain't the same, Brady. And I worry about it."

When Dad went up front to answer a call on the radio, I stood for a long time staring down at the haul we'd made, watching the crabs while they blew bubbles and snapped at one another. I remember thinking how pretty they were with their moist olive green shells and that bright blue stripe down their claws. And I had the odd thought about how this was the end for them. There would be no more second chances. No more swimming in the beautiful bay or up the Corsica River. They'd be in somebody's steamer that night.

This was not a normal way to think. Not for me! But a dark sense of dread washed over me, and I almost couldn't breathe. It had nothing to do with the scarcity of crabs or feeling sorry for the bay. No. It was all because of Ben. Ben, who didn't get his second chance. Who wouldn't grow up now. I was suffocating, and no one knew it. I had to do *something!*

So I flipped out—I mean, how else would you explain the fact that all of a sudden I started picking up those baskets and dumping everything back overboard?

CHAPTER TEN

Brady! Stop!" Dad hollered.

But by the time he saw me dumping the crabs, there were only two bushels left.

"What the hell are you doin'?" he demanded, seizing my wrist with one hand and the basket with his other.

I couldn't look at him.

"Brady!"

All I felt was empty inside—empty and removed—as though it wasn't even me who was standing there.

"What's goin' on?" he shouted at me.

I cringed, but I couldn't answer.

Disgusted, Dad threw down my hand and kicked the last two baskets up toward the front of the boat.

I heard him cuss under his breath, but then nothing more.

Silence as we rode home on the boat.

Neither Mom nor Dad knew what to say, or how to start a conversation with me. So I went to my room down the hall and listened to my parents' hushed voices. *Off the deep end . . . I don't know! . . . For cryin' out loud . . . But I'm worried, Tom . . .* Then I heard my mother call Carl and ask him to come over. I waited inside my door, biting my thumbnail. It hit me then how my parents couldn't talk to me. It's like they wanted to help, but they didn't know *how.*

When Mom finished and hung up the phone, I heard her say that Carl had to be in Easton for a meeting, but that he'd stop by on the way.

I was relieved Carl was coming. I changed and waited for him in the kitchen. When he came in, he had my parka, the one I had wrapped around Ben. My mother took it and gave Carl back the jacket the police officer had lent me. It occurred to me she must have quietly gotten rid of Ben's jacket, too. That and his life jacket. I hadn't seen them around the house.

Carl and I pulled out chairs at the kitchen table.

"We're going out to get a pizza," Mom said as she and my father came through the room. "We'll bring it back, Carl, if you want to stay and eat with us—"

"Thanks—I'm all set," Carl replied.

Mom picked up her purse. As Dad put his cap on and opened the door for her, I thought how easy he'd been on me considering what I had done. All that work and he'd brought home a measly two bushels. I began to feel unbelievably stupid and ungrateful for doing that to him—to *us.* What I did affected the whole family.

After my parents were gone, Carl unzipped his brown leather jacket and rested his strong arms on the table. He seemed just a little bit uncomfortable, but I was sure he would say the right thing. Carl is one smart person, and he's got a good heart, too. If anyone had the answer, it was him. I remember once, when Carl worked with the toll facilities police, how he stopped a woman from jumping off the Chesapeake Bay Bridge just by talking to her. He never would tell me exactly what he said. None of those guys are supposed to talk about it. But whatever it was, it must have been good.

So I listened up, even if I didn't *look* up.

Carl pressed his thick fingers together. "You know," he finally began, "every time we get a call, Brady, a car accident or a hunting incident—and somebody dies at the scene— it's very distressing to us."

I lifted my eyes.

"Even though we know someone has died, we keep going back to recheck. To make sure the person has—you know, passed on. It's a little like we can't quite believe it." He shrugged. "Can't quite accept it—because see?" He opened his hands. "Here we have all this training, all this skill, and sometimes it's simply too late. Or for some reason it wasn't meant to be. It wasn't necessarily our fault 'cause we didn't get there in time."

Carl paused. "In the end, there isn't anything more we can do. We need to put it behind us. So we can move on to the next one. If we didn't, we would be totally burned out.

"You need to do the same thing, Brady," he said, waiting until our eyes connected. "You need to talk it out—people have these feelings, you know. You need to talk it out and put it behind you so you can move forward."

I looked away again, but I knew Carl needed me to respond. A little nod was all I could manage. I didn't know how to express what I was feeling, which, as far as I could tell then was a combination of guilt for what I *hadn't* done, anger because of what did happen—and enormous sadness for Ben and his family. Maybe that's what I should have told him.

It took me a while, but I was getting my thoughts together when Carl stood up.

He shouldn't have stood up. Another few seconds, maybe, I could have gotten something out.

"You sure you don't want to talk about it?" he asked. It was obvious he needed to get going because he glanced at his watch.

I nodded again. I didn't want to hold him back.

"Look, I gotta run, Brady, but if you change your mind and want to talk, give me a holler. You know where I am."

I stared at the table, disappointed, while Carl zipped up his jacket.

"Wait," I said when Carl reached for the door handle, because there was one thing I had to know.

He turned around.

"I just wondered what happened. I mean . . . why did Ben die?" I felt my voice quaver. "I thought you guys had a pulse."

Carl came back to the table and sat down. He forced me to look at him.

"We *did* have a pulse, Brady. There is no question you brought him back."

I swallowed hard. I hoped Carl wouldn't think less of me for getting tears in my eyes.

"But he had a lot of water in his lungs, and it gave him pneumonia, what they call aspiration pneumonia," Carl explained. "That on top of the exposure—it was too much."

I dropped my eyes again and was trying real hard to hold everything in.

Carl cleared his throat a little. "He went fast, they tell me. Kids, when they go down, they go fast."

I wiped at my eyes with the heel of my hand.

"Don't beat yourself, Brady," Carl said. "You did a great thing. You *tried*. You gave it your best, and that's what matters."

Carl ended up staying until my parents came back with the pizza, but then he left. Mom and Dad still seemed worried about me. Dad even said I could hang out at home again the next day if I wanted. But I guess the talk with Carl did me a little good after all because what I said was, "Thanks, but it's time to move on."

I tried. I tried the best I could. In my room, I put away the bag of LEGOs and slid my heavy backpack over to my desk. I took a shower, reviewed material for the social studies exam I had missed, and hung a clean shirt on the drawer pull of my bureau.

But at school the next day, I couldn't seem to pick up where I had left off. I knew I avoided looking at people. I just wanted to be invisible, but I couldn't because a lot of kids came up to me and said they were sorry and "it's too bad about what happened."

They were just being nice, I know. But I couldn't think of what to say back. Plus, I didn't feel as though I belonged in school that day. Everyone else was in a good mood because of it being Friday, and spring break was the following week. But I just wanted to find J.T. Then I wanted to be left alone.

I waited for J.T. at his locker during six-minute break, but he never showed up, so I went on to social studies by myself, knowing I'd see him there, in class. I was supposed to sleep over J.T.'s house that night, only I was thinking of backing out on him because I wasn't up for it. Then again, I thought, it might be good to watch a movie and play a bunch of video games and stuff. I didn't know. I was mixed up. So when I saw J.T. finally come through the door, I was relieved.

"Hey," I said, when J.T. took the seat beside me, where he always sits.

"How ya doin'?" he asked.

"Not so good, I replied, rolling my eyes. "It's been really awful."

J.T. nodded. "I'll bet."

I thought he was going to say something else, but he didn't. He sort of paused, then reached into his backpack and pulled a book up onto his desk. He started looking through it, like he was searching for homework or something. But we didn't have any that I knew of.

"J.T.," I said. "About tonight—"

"Tonight?"

"Yeah. You wanted me to come over, remember?"

"Oh—gee," he replied, before getting this weird look. Like he just remembered something. "Tonight—Brady, I don't think we can do it."

"No big deal," I said, trying to make light of it. After all, I was relieved. Wasn't I?

"We've got all next week off," I said. "We can do something later."

J.T. shot a quick glance at me. "Actually, we won't be home. We're going down to North Carolina—to visit my aunt and uncle."

I stared at him because J.T.'s family hardly ever went anywhere, on account of their chicken farm.

He must have known what I was thinking. "My dad's not going."

Just then, our teacher, Mr. Figley, came in the room and loudly closed the door so we'd all shut up.

After class, I spoke briefly with Mr. Figley about making up the test I had missed, then I tried to catch up with J.T., just for the walk downstairs—he went to Spanish and I went to math. But he had slipped into the crowd and disappeared.

Later, in the hall between third and fourth periods, I saw Digger, and I know he saw me—because I watched him do a double take and then turn a complete one-eighty.

Then, back at my locker, where I stopped to switch books, Kate came up to me. She was still on crutches because of her ankle, so her girlfriend Ryan carried her backpack.

"Sorry about Ben," she said.

"Me, too. It's really sad," Ryan added.

"Thanks," I muttered.

Kate had her brown hair pulled up and back into two ponytails, like a little kid. But it was cute.

When I bent down to pick up my books, she said, "I guess I'll see you tonight. Mom said you were coming over."

Surprised, I straightened up. "I thought you were going to North Carolina."

Kate's eyes widened. "What are you talking about?"

"J.T. said—" And it hit me fast. J.T. had made up the story because he didn't *want* me over. "I'm confused," I mumbled, scrambling to figure out why. "I guess I got it mixed up."

Ryan was nudging Kate.

"Yeah, we have to go," Kate said. "See you, Brady."

"See ya," I said. But as she hobbled away with Ryan, I stood there wondering: Why would J.T. lie to me? And why would Digger not even want to talk to me?

I needed to get to class. Lockers slammed. Everyone was hustling. Ernie Bodkin knocked my shoulder as he rushed by. But I stood there, staring.

I didn't get it.

The bell rang. I was going to be late. But I didn't much care because I just didn't get it.

CHAPTER ELEVEN

There was a funeral for Ben a couple days later. A friend of the DiAngelos called to invite us. The funeral was out in Leesburg, Virginia, where they're from. But I didn't want to go.

My parents said that was fine. They said they understood if I didn't want to go. But I think Mom worried about me. The day of the funeral she asked me to drive into Centreville with her to help with the grocery shopping and errands. And she took me to lunch at Pizza Hut, and we almost never eat lunch out.

I could feel her keeping an eye on me while I played with the straw in my soda. Pushing her salad plate to the side, Mom picked up her coffee and said, "Brady, you need to put this behind you and move forward."

Her words echoed Carl's.

"I know," I agreed. But how did you do that? Every day I kept thinking about what had happened on the river, and I couldn't seem to get the traction I needed for forward motion.

"Do you want to take the rest home?" Mom asked gently.

I stared at the uneaten half of my small pizza not caring, but I nodded because we never waste food.

Across the street, Mom pulled into a parking place at the new shopping center my father hated because it had sprung up in what used to be a cornfield where he went hunting as a kid. I wasn't particular; in fact, I never minded an excuse to go anywhere outside of our town—if you can call it that. All we have at Bailey's Wharf is a crossroads near school where there's a post office and the firehouse, a gas station that sells bait, a video store, and the 7-Eleven.

"You all right?" Mom asked, pulling the keys out of the ignition.

"Yeah."

She handed me a piece of paper with the things Dad needed from the hardware store and a twenty-dollar bill. "I'll meet you back here in half an hour, okay?"

When I finished buying the clamps and sandpaper Dad needed, I saw that I still had twenty minutes before meeting Mom, so I drifted into the Dollar Store to poke around and remembered I needed batteries for my CD player. Some little kids were in the store, examining the new Spider-Man action figure, seeing what it could do. I thought of Ben, and I couldn't help myself. I tried to imagine what his funeral was like. I had never been to a funeral. Not even Amanda's. Carl took me up to the National Aquarium in Baltimore the day they buried my sister, and I didn't know until it was over.

I'm sure my parents thought they were protecting me, but I always felt cheated. Like it left yet another hole in my life. It irritates me even now when I think of how I rode all those escalators to see a bunch of fancy sea horses and polka-dotted fish when I could have been saying good-bye to Amanda one last time. This is the truth: After that, I never once wanted to go back to that aquarium, not even when fourth grade went there on a field trip. Mom never knew it, but I faked a stomachache that day.

"Excuse me. Are you okay?" the woman behind the register narrowed her eyes as she peered at me. I must have looked kind of spaced-out.

"No, I don't think so," I mumbled, turning to walk out and forgetting all about the batteries.

After we got home that day, it started raining again. It rained practically the entire spring vacation.

During that break, I worked on a term paper for English and hoped that J.T. or Digger would call. They didn't. At the end of the week, Carl asked me to go with him while he took his mother, my aunt Tracy, who doesn't drive, down to Richmond so she could stay for a few days and help her dad move into a nursing home. Even though we're cousins, I had never met Carl's other grandfather before. He's real old now and has that disease where you forget. He didn't even know Carl or my aunt when we walked in. "It's *me, Tracy*," my aunt told him. "Your daughter!" she said, opening her arms for a hug. But Carl's grandfather didn't recognize her and even backed away, knocking a chair over.

For hours, we packed up boxes for Carl's grandfather. All

his sweaters and socks and towels. Even his silverware and his coffee mugs. Carl's grandfather watched game shows on television the whole time, except when he occasionally got up to tell us we needed to hurry because he was late for work. Afterward, we ordered some Chinese food and spent the night, Aunt Tracy in the guest room, Carl on the couch, and me on a funky futon thing his grandfather had.

The next morning, other relatives were coming to help. Carl had to get back for his shift, though, so he and I got up early and left. We drove through a Burger King for breakfast, then got right back on Route 301 and drove north.

"I feel sorry for your mom," I told Carl. "It's going to be a hard week for her."

"Yeah. But you know Mom, Brady. She wouldn't be happy if she wasn't helping someone."

True, I thought. My aunt Tracy had a heart of gold. And, if you asked me, so did Carl, the way he was always helping her—*and* us.

It started me thinking that maybe there was more *I* could be doing. Like for the DiAngelos.

By the time we got back from Richmond, it had stopped raining, and even though we'd only been gone for a day, it seemed as if spring had suddenly moved into Maryland. Clusters of daffodils and pudgy little purple hyacinths had sprouted up all over our yard. The ground was squishy from water, and behind the house, where Mom had started raking out her butterfly garden, the earthy scent of marsh drifted up from the river.

That evening Mom fried a rockfish and served one of her applesauce cakes for dessert. It was a nice dinner. You could tell we were all trying to make a fresh start and get things back to normal.

"Anything happen while I was gone?" I asked, digging into my cake.

"Well, let's see." Dad scratched his head. "The locusts are in bloom, so that means the crabs is havin' their first molt. See, too, that Mr. Hennessey down the road planted his soybean field."

Mom smiled and lifted her eyebrows. "Uncle Henry brought me a bag of manure for the garden."

I snorted. "Okay. What I meant is did anything exciting happen?"

Mom and Dad looked at each other.

"Like did anyone call?" I prodded.

"Yes!" Mom replied. "Your aunt Janet called from Rhode Island. She wants you to go up and spend a week with them when school gets out."

I knew they'd contrived the trip to get my mind off things.

I half smiled. "Anyone else?"

Slowly, Mom shook her head. "No, I don't think so."

Neither J.T. nor Digger had called, then. I felt my heart dip. The whole week had passed and neither one of them had called.

"It rained the entire time you were gone," Mom reminded me. Like maybe that was an excuse. But on rainy days, the three of us had some of our best times down in J.T.'s basement. His family had one of those big-screen TVs and an air-hockey table, too.

I cut a big forkful of cake and pushed it into my mouth with a lot of resolve behind it. Good friends wouldn't ignore me like this, I thought. I wasn't going to let those guys get to me. And in the meantime, I'd show Ben's family just how sorry I was about what had happened.

After I swallowed, I announced, "I'm going to offer my help to the DiAngelos."

My parents seemed surprised. Dad shrugged. "Great idea," he said.

"What kind of help?" Mom wanted to know.

"Anything. Rake the yard. Mow the lawn. Whatever they need."

Mom appeared thoughtful as she stirred her tea. "I heard from someone at the grocery store that Gina—Mrs. DiAngelo—is over there by herself," she said. "I'm sure she'd appreciate your offer."

"What do you mean? 'Mrs. DiAngelo is over there by herself.' Where's Mr. DiAngelo?" I asked.

Mom kept stirring her tea. "They have an apartment in northern Virginia. Maybe he's staying there."

I stopped eating. "I don't get it. Why would she be there alone?"

It was getting a little tense in our dining room. I looked from Mom to Dad, and back to Mom again.

She set her spoon down on her saucer. "Sometimes," she said gingerly, "when there's been a death, it drives a family apart, instead of together."

At first, that didn't make a lick of sense to me. You'd think people would hold tight after a tragedy like the one with Ben. But then, I only had to think back on what happened to my sister and watch Mom bite her lip to realize it didn't always work that way.

My father got up and left. This was *way* past his comfort level.

Mom reached over to touch my hand. "They need some time, Brady. And maybe what they need right now is time apart."

After I heard Mrs. DiAngelo was over there alone, I was more determined than ever to help her. So the next day, Sunday, I asked Mom for her help, and we made a spinach lasagna and put the ingredients for a spicy Italian bread into the bread machine. I didn't mind the cooking. I felt as though I was an old hand in the kitchen—ever since those days at the fire station. Even so, I made one heck of a mess spilling flour all over the place, including on Tilly, because she was right under my feet the whole time.

As soon as the bread machine beeped, I pulled the loaf out, wrapped it in tinfoil, and put it in a cardboard box with the tray of lasagna. Mom had also picked a thick bunch of daffodils, which she put in a coffee can with water and nestled into a corner of the box. On top, I settled a folded note, offering my help. I signed my name and left a phone number and an e-mail address.

Mom had done so much of the work I wanted her to

come, too. But at the last minute she said she couldn't, and Dad took me.

The box was warm on my lap. I was proud of what Mom and I had created. Halfway up the DiAngelos' driveway, though, I had a terrible thought: What if Mrs. DiAngelo didn't want visitors? And me in particular? What if she closed the door in my face? What if she didn't know how hard I tried to save Ben?

The DiAngelos' driveway is pretty long, winding across the field where J.T., Digger, and I used to shoot tin cans, so there was a lot of time for me to agonize over this. When the DiAngelos' huge brick house came into view, Dad slowed his pickup and parked behind a new black Saab. The DiAngelos had four cars, including a silver Porsche, that J.T. lusted after. I didn't see the Porsche though. Maybe Mr. DiAngelo had it, over at that apartment in Virginia.

We rang the doorbell a few times and waited at least ten minutes, but no one ever came. Disappointed, we set the box by the door and left.

Dad didn't say anything on the drive back home. Not that it's unusual for Dad to be quiet. But I could tell something was eating at him. When we walked into the kitchen, where Mom was unloading the dishwasher, he finally told me.

"Look, Brady," he began, "I know it's been hard. But it's time to be gettin' on. I got way too much to do to take on your chores, too."

Mom held a stack of plates. The room grew quiet.

"Either do something with those crab pots tomorrow or pull 'em in," Dad said.

I hadn't thought a lick about crabbing. Not a lick! Even if I didn't rebait them, I knew I needed to move the pots around. If you don't—sometimes on Dad's boat we even hose them off—they'll gunk up and disintegrate.

Dad turned the cap in his hands. "One other thing," he went on. "I know you kids must've been in my shop sometime over the past few weeks and took my drill. The cordless one—the one runs on batteries? I can't find it anywhere, and I need it."

"We didn't take it, Dad. I know we didn't," I insisted, hurt because I'm good about putting things back. Especially if it was something from his shop.

My father let out his breath, like he didn't believe me. Then he set his cap and truck keys on the counter and left.

Mom could tell Dad had hurt my feelings. In a soft voice she explained how he'd been under some pressure lately to join the other watermen in a protest against the state's new crabbing regulations. "They're talking about petitioning the governor and demonstrating over in Annapolis," she said.

"And Dad doesn't want to do it?"

She made a face and shrugged. "He's been kind of funny about it. Like he's not sure. But I don't see how he can't go along with the others. It's his livelihood, Brady. It's what puts food on this table."

I stood, staring down the hallway after my dad. I hated to let my father down. *Hated* it. Especially if he was having problems of his own. So I set my alarm for 4 A.M. in order to check my crab pots before school, then laid out my clothes for the morning. I even made two peanut-butter-and-honey sandwiches and left them in the refrigerator beside a bottle of Gatorade so I could grab them on my way out the door.

It was brutal when that buzzer went off. I moaned and pushed the warm covers off. On automatic pilot I got dressed and let Tilly out. Then I shoved the sandwiches in my coat pocket, grabbed the Gatorade, and scooped up the flashlight at the end of the counter.

The house was silent. Monday was Dad's day to work in the shop, so he and Mom wouldn't be up for another two hours.

Outside the toolshed, I picked up a basket to fill with razor clams from the refrigerator. But even before I opened the door to fetch the bait, I could feel how something had shut down inside of me.

With the empty basket still in my hand, I walked along the short path to the dock. By then, my eyes had adjusted to the dark. I flicked the flashlight off and stood there, staring out over the creek. Tilly had hopped into my boat and was waiting.

But I knew I couldn't go back out on the water. Not because I was afraid, or because I blamed the river for what happened. It was because of an overwhelming sadness that came over me being near the water. In the hazy morning air, all I could see was a red kayak, sunk in the river, and Ben's half-closed eyes and cold blue lips. Whatever it was inside of me that had shut down curled inward.

In the kitchen, I left a note for Dad saying my engine was broke, and went back to bed. Tilly seemed to understand and lay quietly on the rug beside me.

Later that day, when I got home from school, Dad told me two terrapins had drowned in my pots. I wondered how he knew. But walking out back, I could see that my father had pulled every one of my traps and stacked them up, four deep, behind the shed.

sometimes wonder what would have happened if Mrs. DiAngelo hadn't sent me that e-mail the next day. Because I was on a downward spiral—no question—and that e-mail changed everything.

> Brady—
> I'm sorry I didn't thank you earlier for the lasagna and the flowers. I appreciated it so much. It's been diffi-cult. And I never even thanked you for what you did. It is so generous of you to offer to help. I do need someone to help with the yard. Would you like a summer job?
> Gina DiAngelo

It was never my intention to get a summer job out of Mrs. DiAngelo. But I went over on Saturday to talk about it. Mom dropped me off. She'd made some cranberry-orange muf-fins that morning, so I brought a paper plate with six of them covered in plastic wrap.

When I rang the doorbell and watched my mother drive off, I didn't even think about being on that porch a few days ago with the lasagna dinner. Instead, I stood there recalling the very first time we'd come as a family, the new neighbors, to the DiAngelos for dinner. This would have been during the holidays, five months earlier, because I remembered the porch banisters all decorated with pine boughs and an enormous, sweet-smelling bayberry wreath that hung on the front door.

Dad hadn't been too keen on the dinner idea because, for starters, he's suspicious of all these rich new people moving onto the shore, buying up our farmland, riprapping the waterfront, and building their mansions with three-car garages. Plus he hates "gettin' fancy." He'd kept muttering, "I'm not even gonna know which durn fork to use." But Dad didn't have any trouble with his forks that night. And he had everybody hooked and laughing at his stories about the good old days.

Mr. DiAngelo didn't believe Dad when he told him the underwater grasses were so thick when Dad was a boy that he once dragged a box spring through the creek to clear a channel for his boat. And Mrs. DiAngelo seemed delighted with all of us as she swung her head back and forth, talking to Mom and me across the table and tending to Ben, who sat beside her in his booster seat, smashing peas and potatoes in his face and making one heck of a mess.

Mom was pretty that night, with her sparkly earrings and her long, sandy-colored hair twisted up on her head. We kept catching each other's eye, chuckling over the things

Ben said. Such as, "This cawwot is a topeedo—watch!" as he made the vegetable plow a path through the gravy on his plate before targeting his mouth.

After dessert, after I'd picked up every morsel of that delicious key-lime pie with my fork tines, I said to Ben, "Hey. How about showing me that new hamster you got for Christmas?"

"Oh, Ben! Did you hear that? Brady wants to see Tiny Tim!" Mrs. DiAngelo exclaimed. I could tell she was very appreciative. While she lifted Ben out of his booster seat, Mr. DiAngelo poured more wine for the adults, and I caught a grateful look from my parents as well.

Ben's hamster was cute and had an incredible setup with a big cage and all kinds of connecting plastic tubes and hideouts. Plus he had an exercise wheel and a glow ball he could run inside.

"You got to be kidding me," I said when Ben explained how the glow ball rolled around on the floor.

Fearless, Ben scooped up the hamster with one hand, plopped him inside that ball, and snapped the little door closed. Then he ran to the light switch and turned out the lights so we could sit cross-legged on Ben's bed-that-looked-like-a-race-car and watch the ball glow and roll around the bedroom floor. It was surreal, but I'll tell you, I about died laughing.

I had time to think back on all this because it was taking Mrs. DiAngelo an age to answer the door. Suddenly, though, I heard footsteps and the sound of the lock being turned from the inside.

"Brady," Mrs. DiAngelo said, opening the door.

I hoped it wasn't rude the way I dropped my mouth, but I almost didn't recognize her she looked so bad. Like a bedraggled ghost, you could say. Her skin was pale as chalk and her eyes puffy with big, dark bags underneath. Even her hair, usually so thick and curly, was pulled back severely, held at the nape of her neck with a cloth scrunchie like a lot of the girls wear at school.

"Come in," she said, stepping back.

I brushed off my baseball cap as I entered.

She smiled a little when she took the muffins. Since she was dressed in sweatpants and an oversize flannel shirt, I thought maybe we'd go straight to the yard to start working, but she led me through the house to the kitchen.

The DiAngelos' kitchen is twice the size of our living room, with its own fireplace and glass doors that open onto a patio. There's a spectacular view overlooking the creek. I glanced at it—you can't help it—but mostly I was keeping an eye on Mrs. DiAngelo, hoping she wouldn't get too sad or anything.

"I do want to thank you," she said.

I knew she didn't mean the muffins.

"It was no trouble," I replied, immediately thinking how stupid that sounded. "I mean that I did my best, Mrs. DiAngelo."

"I'm sure you did, Brady." She sat and looked out the window.

Unzipping my jacket, I sat down, too. But it was awkward. I didn't feel as though I had said enough, or the right thing.

And you could *feel* her sorrow. It filled every molecule of air in that room. But man, I did not know what to say! Somehow, we laid out a plan for me coming over to take care of the yard. And even though I'd told her I just wanted to help, she insisted on paying me, and I agreed. I agreed with everything because I didn't want to argue with her.

That afternoon, I began work by cutting the lawn, which took me about four hours with their riding lawn mower. When I was finished, Mrs. DiAngelo fed me lunch—a sandwich, chips, and lemonade—on her patio. Then she asked if I would take Ben's hamster.

"Take him. You mean keep him?" I asked.

She nodded quickly, and I could see her eyes filling up.

"Sure—oh, it's fine!" I assured her, realizing how Tiny Tim must be a constant reminder of Ben. "I'll take him right now, if you want."

We strode silently, the two of us, through the house to Ben's room upstairs. The door was closed, and we stopped outside of it.

"I can't go in, Brady. But here—" She thrust some money into my hands. "For food and things that he needs."

I looked at the money, a thick wad of folded bills.

"Please," she repeated. "I'll get my car and meet you out front, okay?"

She turned and moved quickly down the stairs. I heard her clogs clomp across the marble foyer, then the front door open and close. Only then did I stuff the money in my pocket and turn the doorknob to enter Ben's room.

It was just as I remembered it from when I baby-sat

several weeks ago. There were LEGOs all over the place, including part of the castle we'd built. A wooden train was set up. The car bed was neatly made, with a stuffed dinosaur leaning against the pillow, which was in the shape of a tire. Pajamas were laid out on the bed. And a pair of fuzzy duck slippers sat waiting on the floor.

I felt extremely sad being in that room. I could understand why Mrs. DiAngelo didn't want to go in. The hamster was beginning to smell, too. Only then did I wonder what my mother was going to say when I walked in with a hamster. A *rodent*.

At home, I set the hamster cage on a newspaper-covered card table in my room. Tilly was delighted to have Tiny Tim with us, and Mom didn't care, it turned out. "Just keep it clean," she warned. But the first night the hamster made so much noise running around in his wheel that I had to move him down to the basement. How could Ben stand all that racket? I wondered. As it was, I still had trouble sleeping.

I threw myself into working for Mrs. DiAngelo. After school. Saturdays. Sometimes, when I arrived on the weekend, she wasn't even out of bed. She hid a key in the garage so I could get into the house to use the bathroom or get a drink, and one morning, when I let myself in, I heard her upstairs throwing up. I worried she was making herself sick from being so depressed, and so alone. Her mother, her sister, a friend—they'd all come and gone. But I was afraid to talk to her and so just kept myself busy.

And boy, there was plenty to do at the DiAngelos' place.

Every other week I mowed the lawn and trimmed, which took all day. Then I mulched the gardens, weeded, planted, and watered everything. She had a whole truckload of stuff delivered: impatiens, marigolds, geraniums, miniature roses. She showed me where she wanted everything planted, and the day she stood there, pointing around at her garden, was the first time she seemed just a little bit better.

I guess I got caught up in the moment. "You get a lot of sun here. You ought to plant yourself a butterfly garden— like my mom," I suggested.

"A butterfly garden," she repeated, like it was a real enchanting idea.

She crossed her arms, thinking, while I dug a hole fo one of the rosebushes. "We get a lot of butterflies," I sai angling the shovel.

"There are certain plants, then, that they like?"

"Oh! Are you kidding?" I had to stop for a second expound a little, because I knew a lot about butter "First off, they don't like red. They like yellow and pu and blue the best."

"Really?"

"Clusters, too," I said, encouraged by her intere know, as opposed to, like, a single plant. And th some flat rocks—so they can warm up before t off. Plus a low-lying source of water. You could pu pad pond or just a birdbath if you didn't want to trouble."

She glanced around the yard. "How about by

"Perfect! Any place that gets a lot of sun."

I grinned and went back to digging.

"How long has your mom had a butterfly garden?" she asked.

I had to stop and think. "Six years," I replied, dumping the earth beside the hole. "Ever since my sister died."

Boy, I knew the instant I said it that I shouldn't have because it would make her think of Ben. And there I was— *digging holes!* Warily, I looked up.

Mrs. DiAngelo looked startled. "You lost a sister, Brady?"

"Yeah," I acknowledged with a sigh. "When she was five months old."

She put a hand up on her chest.

"It's okay now!" I rushed to assure her, even though it wasn't really true. "I mean that it was a long time ago. And the butterfly garden has helped."

Her wide, mournful eyes had settled on me, and I could tell they weren't going anywhere until I explained that a little better.

"Mom—my mom—she believes that butterflies are like little spirits. Who knows? Maybe even my sister's," I said, shrugging because I'd never been sure about that.

Mrs. DiAngelo nodded. "Would you excuse me, Brady?" she said before rushing off.

I kicked the shovel because I knew I'd stirred things up. I wondered if she'd want me back after that. But she did. She then started asking me what I liked for sandwiches and drinks, and at noon, she'd sit down with me to chitchat for a few minutes while I ate. One day, we talked about butterflies again, and I told her about butterfly eyes.

"They can look forward and backward at the same time," I said. "It's true because they have hundreds of separate lenses. It's like looking out from a bowl—a fish-eye, panoramic view of the world."

Her dark eyes sparkled.

"You don't believe me? Try sneaking up on a butterfly!" I challenged her.

"Oh, I believe you!"

I have to say, it was terrific to see her smile again even if she did still look pretty run-down.

Digger was still being a total jerk, avoiding me. But J.T. started talking to me in school. "We need to get together," he kept saying. But neither one of us picked up the phone. I was busy, and I figured he was, too, working his butt off on that chicken farm after school—plus we had final exams coming up. It's funny. Even though I came home exhausted every day that I worked for Mrs. DiAngelo, I was getting some of my old energy back. Evenings, I threw the ball for Tilly, helped Dad repair some of his broken crab pots, and even offered to help my mother with the dishes one night when it wasn't my turn.

"Mrs. DiAngelo is curious about your garden," I told Mom as I plunged my hands into the soapy water.

My mother was putting leftovers away. "She is?"

"Yeah, she's been reading up on it. Just today she asked about your foundation shrubs. So I told her about the butterfly bush and that smaller one, the purple one."

"Lavender," Mom gently reminded me as she snapped

the lid on a bowl of leftover coleslaw. "Lots of different shrubs would work, though: azaleas, rhododendrons, spice-bush—a wisteria vine."

"*Mom,* I told her about the butterfly bush and the lavender because they get a lot of butterflies. I didn't know all the other names. *You* do, though. Maybe *you* could go over one day and give her some advice."

"Me?" Mom put the bowl in the refrigerator and stood, closing the door, with her back to me.

"Yeah, *you,* Mom. It might be nice. I mean, no one ever goes to see her. A couple of people from her church now and then. But they don't stay long." I rinsed a pot and set it in the dish drainer.

She turned around. "Marcellus hasn't come back?"

"No. She even told me one day he blames her for what happened."

Mom winced. "She did?"

"Yeah, I guess she wanted me to know why he wasn't there. I feel sorry for her because she's so alone. She spends the first half of the day in bed, then she just sort of goes through the motions the rest of the day."

Mom retrieved a basket from the table and put the left-over rolls in a Ziploc bag. "The poor thing, she must be so depressed."

"I don't know about depressed," I said, scrubbing hard on a blackened skillet. "But she sure is sick a lot. Almost every morning she throws up—"

"Brady!" Mom swung around to look at me.

"What?"

"Is Mrs. DiAngelo pregnant?"

I stopped scrubbing. "How would I know?!"

Mom's eyes flitted sideways. She ran a hand back through her hair. "I'm sorry. Of course you wouldn't know. But those are pretty classic symptoms, you know—morning nausea, fatigue."

I didn't say anything. Just went back to cleaning that skillet.

"Well, is there something you can do for her?" Mom persisted.

That's what got me. I stopped scrubbing and turned around to confront my mother. "I don't know what more I can do, but you know what? Maybe *you* could try to help her, too. I mean, gee whiz—you're a mother! You lost a kid! You have things to say to her that I can't!"

Never had I spoken to my mother like that before. Never. I let my breath out and stared at the faucets, then rested my wrists on the edge of the sink, bracing myself for Mom's angry reaction. But it never came.

"You're right," Mom said quietly. She wiped her hands on a dish towel. "I should go see her." She untied her apron, folded it, and set it on the counter. "I should go see her right now."

And I watched her go.

Across the kitchen. And out the door.

I don't know what Mom said, but I do know this: A few days later, Mrs. DiAngelo had one fine butterfly garden out there by her pool. I know because I planted it! She had a butterfly bush and yellow sunflowers, cosmos, daisies, daylilies, two birdbaths full of water. I even planted some milkweed, violets, and wispy salt grass for the caterpillars— you know, when butterflies are in the larval stage. Then I bordered all of it with dozens of miniature marigolds.

Not that I was keeping track, but it had been six weeks since Ben died, and I was beginning to feel things shift just a little for the better.

At the end of May, the Saturday of Memorial Day weekend, I planned on working a few hours for Mrs. DiAngelo, then I was going to knock off early and go to a picnic at my uncle Henry's. Get this—I was even thinking of asking J.T. to come with us.

Memorial Day weekend. I'll never forget it. Because just when things started to come back together, they came undone in a Big Way.

CHAPTER THIRTEEN

t was a hot day, that Saturday. I had mowed the lawn the weekend before, so Mrs. DiAngelo said she had something else for me to do. "Down at the dock," she said, "there's a lovely old boathouse that we've never cleaned out."

She didn't realize that I knew the old boathouse like the back of my hand. When Digger's grandfather owned the property, J.T., Digger, and I played pirates in that boathouse and used our dinghy for the pirate ship.

"I wondered if you could get things into some kind of order," Mrs. DiAngelo said. "Pull everything out, sort it. If there's anything salvageable, put it aside. Make a pile for the dump. Then just rake up around there. It's such a mess."

"Sure," I replied.

"Another thing," she said. "I'll be away for a couple of days."

"You will?" I was surprised.

"Yes." She started to smile. "Thanks to your mother. She's the one who talked a little sense into me. I'm going in to

Washington. My husband and I have been talking. We need to figure out what we're going to do."

I was confused.

"What I mean," she explained, "is that there is another baby on the way and we need to prepare for that."

"A baby?" I was stunned.

She dropped her eyes. "We'll never get over what happened, Brady. Never." Looking up at me, she added, "But life does go on."

I must have stood there with my mouth hanging open because Mrs. DiAngelo slowly grinned at my reaction. "Your mother knows about the baby. Now you do, too."

"Wow. I mean con-congratulations," I stammered. Truly, I was happy for her. "That's *really* good news!"

"Yes." She glanced around her. "Well. Anyway—Brady, would you mind just coming over and checking on things while I'm gone?"

"Not at all."

"You could turn the sprinkler on one evening, maybe. And take the mail and newspapers in. I'll be away until Tuesday."

"No problem," I said, beaming. "It's no problem at all."

She touched my arm. "Thanks. You've been such a help to me."

I took a rake and a couple big garbage bags and headed on down the hill behind the three-car garage to the dock. The DiAngelos' sailboat bobbed nearby in its slip, and their powerboat sat gleaming on a boat lift beside it. On shore was a dark green canoe, flipped over. And off toward some bushes were two wooden sawhorses, a few feet apart. The sawhorses were where Mr. DiAngelo had rested the red kayak when it was out of the water.

Opening the door to the boathouse, I stepped inside. Besides a lot of dust, a bunch of old memories drifted around me. Not just the pirate games we used to play, but the morning J.T. cut his knee on a piece of broken glass and had to get stitches. And the time Digger ran away from home and made a bed for himself on a bunch of empty grain sacks in one corner. I had to shake my head, remembering how we all brought him food—sandwiches and cookies and stuff, but his sojourn didn't last much beyond dinnertime. When bats started flying around at dusk, he got scared and went on home.

Peering inside a wooden barrel full of bailing twine, I recalled the rope ladders we used to make for our pirate getaways and how one time the flimsy twine ladder broke, sending me into the water with a big splash while J.T. and Digger howled from the dock above.

"Whew!" I needed to plow through the nostalgia and get to work. But where to start? Junk in that boathouse was piled ten feet high. Old wicker lawn furniture, tattered fruit baskets, a large, cracked headboard. Overwhelmed, I decided to clean around the outside first.

Grabbing the rake, I began pulling debris away from the sides of the boathouse. Dried-up leaves, piles of brush, big pieces of plastic from a kids' old swimming pool. It wasn't going to be fun *or* easy, I concluded pretty quickly. But I gritted my teeth and went at it so I could knock off and go home early.

"Good-bye, Brady!" Mrs. DiAngelo called out from the hill. She had sunglasses on, her hair up in a little bun, a tote bag in her hand.

I waved back. "Have a good trip!"

After she left, I went clear down one side of the boathouse, raking, making piles, and periodically stuffing the junk into one of the two black leaf bags. Already sweat was trickling down my face and neck. My hands were slick inside the heavy work gloves I wore. I took them off so my hands could breathe for a while, tossed the gloves on a nearby tree stump, and took a long drink of ice water from the plastic jug I'd brought with me.

Out of the blue, I smiled. Truth was, I was pretty happy about the baby. I knew it wouldn't replace Ben. But it had to help. I started whistling a song I liked from the radio as I went back to work.

It was when I turned the corner on the boathouse and pulled the rake through a tangle of prickers that I saw something reflect the sun. At first I thought it might be a knife, some kind of a silver knife. I stopped whistling. But when I reached over to pull it out of the weeds, I saw it wasn't a knife at all. It was a drill. My father's cordless drill. The one he said he was missing a while back.

I held it and let the rake fall because I could see that there were flecks of red paint on the drill bit. I swallowed hard. Flecks of red that looked as though they might even be the same color as the red kayak.

Was it possible? Instinctively, I looked around to see if someone might be watching me. My heart started pounding.

Did someone drill holes in the kayak to make it sink?

Was it Marcellus? Is that why he had disappeared?

No, I decided pretty quickly. Because if Marcellus did it, why would he use one of my father's tools?

In a sort of daze, but still holding the drill, I stumbled back to the front of the boathouse and sat down on the wooden steps leading up to the door. As I did, my mind raced backward almost an entire year, to when the DiAngelos first bought the property from Digger's grandfather. They had just begun construction on the house, but they had left a canoe onshore, and their sailboat at the dock.

It was early evening that summer day last year. We three—J.T., Digger, and I—had come over to the beach beneath the bluff for a swim. It was the DiAngelos' property, yes, but only the week before it had belonged to Digger's grandfather, and many times we had come to swim in the little cove to cool off. The water was shallow, and the way the beach curved made it private, too.

Digger was down in the dumps that day about his grandfather having to let go of the place, and we could see how it was eating him up. He wouldn't even come in the water with us, but sat on the beach, stewing, while J.T. and I swam around, splashing and dunking each other.

We felt sorry for Digger, though. A little sorry for ourselves, too, I guess, because it meant the end of swimming over there. After coming up onshore, we dried off with the towels we'd brought and aimed a few small rocks toward the

DiAngelos' sailboat. One of the stones Digger threw pinged off the metal mast. "Bastards!" he had cried.

"Hey! I've got an idea," I'd told him, tossing a glance at the sailboat. "Let's get my father's drill and put a few holes in her hull."

"Cool!" J.T. had exclaimed. "Then, when they come for a little day sail, they'll realize they aren't going anywhere!"

Digger had looked at me, but he wasn't laughing. "No. That's stupid. The sailboat would just sink. It's gotta be somethin' worse than that."

"Okay!" I'd said. "Then we can put holes in that canoe instead. What you do is fill the holes back in with this water-based glue my dad has in the workshop, mixed in with some of the residue from what you drilled out so no one can tell. Maybe dab over it with a marker—a green marker. Then, after he's out on the water about thirty minutes, the glue gives way, the water comes in—and he goes swimming!"

Digger had stared past me with an intense look on his face.

"Ouch!" I'd cried because J.T. had suddenly whipped me across the back of my legs with his towel. Grabbing my own towel, I had sprinted after him down the beach.

As I sat on the steps of the boathouse, remembering, goose bumps popped up on my arms, and an awful scenario washed over me like a sudden chill, weakening my muscles and nearly taking my breath away.

"My God," I uttered, staring with horror at the drill in my hands. Did Digger have something to do with sinking the kayak?

CHAPTER FOURTEEN

What was I going to do? In those first paralyzing moments I didn't have a clue, just an increasingly sick feeling in my stomach. Finally, I pushed myself up. I stood and wrapped the drill inside the second, unused leaf bag. The bag was way too big, but I just kept wrapping the drill around and around in it.

I carried it back up the hill to where I parked my bicycle in the shade by the side of the garage. I put the bag-wrapped drill in my backpack and got on my bike. I had to tell someone. But who? Not my parents. Not yet, anyway. J.T., I figured. I would tell J.T. Then, together, we could figure out what to do.

All the way down the DiAngelos' long driveway I pedaled faster and faster as I put more and more of it together. How angry Digger had been at the DiAngelos for buying his grandfather's farm. How he had spit out: *Paddle hard, you sucker!* when he saw the red kayak that morning.

When I hit the paved road I leaned into the turn so hard

I almost spun the bike out of control. You'd have thought I was rushing to report a fire the way I sped down the road.

At J.T.'s driveway, I put on my brakes, then pedaled hard up the long dirt road to his house. I thought about taking the drill and showing him right off. But then decided not to and left it in my backpack with my bike.

My heart was pounding like crazy and I was out of breath as I climbed the wide front steps and stood on his porch, knocking on the door. It was pretty scary to think that one of my friends might have had something to do with Ben dying. And I was beginning to wonder what would happen to Digger if it turned out to be true.

Kate opened the door and caught me off guard with her nice smile. "Hi, Brady!"

"Hey," I said, still breathing hard.

The smell of something baking, something chocolate, wafted up behind her, and I spied J.T.'s cute little sister Kerry peeking around the corner to see who had come.

Kate's smile disappeared. She lowered her voice. "Guess you heard."

"What?" I asked, confused, a little panicked. Did *she* know what *I* knew? Had I missed something?

"My father's in the hospital," she said. "Carl came with the ambulance this morning and took him."

"No—no, I didn't know," I managed to say. "Your *father?*"

Kate nodded. "He passed out at the breakfast table." She indicated with her thumb. "He's back awake now—they called from the hospital. We think it's his kidneys. Remember when he had that really bad attack a year ago?"

I did remember. J.T.'s father was in the hospital for almost a month. I even came over and helped J.T. with his chores after school.

Kate's news blew some of the steam off my anger.

"I'm sorry to hear about your dad," I said. But I wasn't forgetting why I had come. "Is J.T. here?"

"He's culling, down at the chicken houses," she said. "Wouldn't you know it? We had a huge shipment of new chicks yesterday."

"Think it would be okay if I went to see him?" I asked.

"Sure," Kate said, nodding eagerly. "He'd be glad to see you."

"I'll go give him a hand, then," I said.

I went back down the steps and walked across their flat dirt yard, past several outbuildings and the huge grain silos, to the first of four long chicken houses. I hated going inside those things because they were so warm. That and the ammonia smell from the chicken waste was so strong you could hardly breathe. But I was desperate to talk to J.T.

Inside the door to the first house, I peered down the narrow building, but all I saw were thousands of yellow baby chicks peeping up a storm and crowding one another around the feeders. They were actually kind of cute at this stage, so small and fluffy. In a matter of days, though, they'd shed that pale yellow fuzz for tough new white feathers, and in just a few weeks, the chicken people, Perdue or whoever, would be back to collect them.

There were big electric fans droning in the windows to keep the birds cool, but it was just as hot as I remembered.

I scoped out the chicken house as far as I could see, but I didn't spot my friend.

Back outside, I took in deep breaths of fresh air and walked, my feet scuffing up dust, over to the next chicken house. Inside the door, I saw J.T. right away. Wearing a bright red T-shirt, he was about halfway down the building, walking slowly, the chicks parting and making a path as he moved. He had a pillowcase in one hand, and when he bent over occasionally, I knew he was picking out the dead chicks, or the ones that were hobbling around, getting ready to keel over.

As I walked toward him, the chicks scattered at my feet, too. Their high-pitched peeping vibrated in my ears, and the soles of my shoes picked up layers of crappy chicken manure, but it was impossible to avoid.

It wasn't until I was right behind J.T. that he finally noticed me.

When he turned and our eyes met, I could see the pain he had bottled up inside. Because of his dad? The sweat dripping off his face could have been tears for all I knew.

J.T. dropped his eyes. I looked away, too, and when I did, I spotted a dead chick, its little feet twitching, and bent over to pick it up.

"Here," I said, offering it to J.T.

He opened his pillowcase and I placed it inside.

"I've got to talk to you," I said loudly, so he could hear above the din.

He nodded. "Let me finish this house," he replied just as loud.

Together, we waded through the ocean of yellow chicks,

both of us stopping here and there to pick up the dead or dying ones, adding them to the bag.

Outside, we walked over to a compost bin, where J.T. dumped the contents of his pillowcase and made a body count, noting the number on a piece of paper. It was a lousy job, but twice a day, someone at the farm had to do the culling.

"So you heard about my dad?" J.T. asked. He wiped the sweat off his face with the back of one hand.

"Sorry," I said. "How is he?"

J.T. folded up the paper and pushed it into his jeans pocket. "I don't know. We're going to see him after we eat."

"Look," I started, "I know this isn't a good time for you, J.T. But I just discovered—"

"You ever had surgery?" J.T. asked, cutting me off.

"Surgery?" His question—and the bluntness of it—threw me.

"Yeah, you ever been put to sleep?"

Hesitating, I nevertheless answered. "Once," I said, wondering where this was going. "Remember when I tore the cartilage in my knee? During that basketball game back in sixth grade?"

"Oh, yeah," J.T. said, fidgeting with the pencil in his hand. "Anyway, I'm thinking I'll give my father one of my kidneys. If I'm compatible, that is. People at the hospital, they're gonna do a blood test on my mom and me."

I stared at my feet, not sure how to respond, then peered back at J.T. "J.T., I'm sorry about your dad—"

"Yeah, it's awful."

"But you got to listen to me, man," I continued firmly, the urgency returning, "because I need your help."

There was a pause. J.T. was not making eye contact. Still fidgeting with that damned pencil, he asked in a small voice, "What is it?"

"Over at the DiAngelos', where I'm working now? I was down at the boathouse, raking up . . ."

Finally, J.T. looked at me.

"And I found my father's drill."

J.T.'s eyes grew large.

My heart jumped into my throat. "J.T.?"

He didn't say anything, but he took a step backward, like I was going to hit him.

Only something hit *me* instead. "Do you know something about this? J.T.? Did Digger drill holes in that kayak?"

Barely, *barely* I saw J.T. nod his head.

I stared at him, and a terrible expression consumed J.T.'s face. "We didn't mean for Mrs. DiAngelo and Ben to get hurt," he blurted out.

"Holy *shit*, J.T.! You were in on this?"

A screen door slammed, and Kate called us. "Guys! Where are you?"

J.T. threw up both hands at me. "*Please*, Brady! They don't know! Please don't say anything in front of Kate!"

"Why?" I demanded, screwing up my face. "Why'd you do it?"

It was a horrible time for Kate to show up, but she did just then, innocently rounding the corner of the chicken house.

"There you are! Hey!" She put her hands on her hips and

smiled. "Grandma wants to know if you'll stay for dinner, Brady. It's just BLTs and corn because we're going to the hospital after dinner to see Daddy. But you're welcome to stay."

J.T. and I glanced at each other.

"I made brownies," Kate chimed sweetly, trying to entice me to have dinner with them.

"Sure—why don't you?" J.T. said in an uncertain voice. His hand, the one holding the pencil, was shaking.

"I can't," I declared, angry beyond words at J.T. and Digger and trying real hard not to show it. Some friends *they* were, I thought. "I've gotta go. In fact, I'm late already. Tell your grandmother I'm sorry, Kate."

I walked away, but when J.T. tried to stop me—"Hey, Brady!"—I started running. When I got to my bike, J.T. was right behind me, breathing hard.

"Don't go to Digger's!" he told me, grabbing my arm. "Don't go without me."

"Why?"

"Because I want to be there, and I can't go right now."

I yanked my arm away. "I can't believe you guys did it. Why? What the hell were you thinking, J.T.?!"

"It was a *mistake!*" J.T. exclaimed.

"Yoo-hoo! Boys!" J.T.'s grandmother waved her handkerchief and called to us from the front steps. "J.T., can't you convince Braden to stay?"

When J.T. looked back at his grandmother, I jumped on my bicycle and tore out of there. Straight for Digger's house.

CHAPTER FIFTEEN

Digger was in his front yard, shooting baskets with his little brother, Hank, when I skidded to a halt on my bike. But Hank was the only one who seemed happy to see me. "Hey, Brady, watch this!" he called out as he bounced the ball off a rusted and netless basket rim.

Lowering my bike to its side, I took off my backpack and set it on the wheel, my eyes fixed on Digger, who was retrieving the basketball and still hadn't said a word. Did he suspect something? Had he been dreading this moment for a long time?

When I started walking toward him, Digger gave the ball to Hank and said, "Go on inside, okay?"

Hank didn't argue. Hank never argued with Digger because he looked up to him too much. He bounced the basketball once and left.

Digger hooked his thumbs in the front pockets of his jeans. "What's up?" he asked, kind of squinting his eyes at me.

He suspected why I was there, I thought. And I stopped,

hesitating. All those years we'd known each other—all the laughs we had, the plans we shared, the trouble we got into—spun by in a blur. But I realized we could never go back to the way it was. Already, the friendship had changed.

"You know I'm working at the DiAngelos now, right?" I asked.

Digger just kept staring at me.

"Well, I found something over there today when I was raking up near the boathouse."

His expression didn't change, but I saw Digger's chin lift up a little.

"I found my dad's drill."

Digger arched his eyebrows. "So?"

"So I am wondering how it got there!" I shot back, ticked off that he was making this difficult. "I'm wondering why it has flecks of red paint on it!"

Digger swallowed.

We locked eyes.

"Beats me," he said.

"Come *on!*" I argued. "We both know what you did. J.T.'s already told me."

Digger frowned and his lips parted as a scared, hurt look softened his steely expression. I was sure he'd admit to it then.

"Where is it?" he asked. "Where's the drill?"

"Back there," I lied. "I left it where I found it. Why? What do you care?"

"I *don't* care!" Digger snapped, toughening up again. "And I don't know what you're gettin' at, Brady."

We stared at each other for a few seconds.

"I gotta go," Digger said, pulling his thumbs from his pockets and turning away while I stood there like an idiot, watching him.

"Digger!" I called out.

Faster and faster he walked, but he never looked back. When the screen door slammed, I kicked at a stone and stomped back to where my bike lay on the ground. Tossing the backpack on, I yanked up the bicycle and hopped on, kicking hard at the pedals. I worried that I was being a coward, letting him walk away the way he did. Questions hammered at me: Should I turn around and force him to admit it? How? How would I do that? Should I tell my parents? Should we call the police?

I didn't know, so I kept on pedaling. When I got to the road, I headed for home.

Riding up our driveway, I saw that Mom's car was gone. Under a flowerpot, I scooped up the hidden key for the side door and let myself in. The house was silent except for Tilly's toenails clicking down the tiled hallway as she came to greet me. I saw on the counter a lemon cake my mother had made for the Memorial Day picnic. Tilly licked my hands, and I touched her on the head before letting her out the back door.

Next thing I did was take the drill out of my backpack and hide it because I was mixed up. Afraid one minute, angry the next. I needed time to think. In the basement, I opened up a cupboard underneath Dad's workbench and pulled out a boxful of rags. Lifting a handful of old curtains, I stashed the drill deep down at the bottom, then pushed the box back underneath.

Tiny Tim, on a shelf nearby, heard me and crawled out of his newspaper nest, so I let him sniff my finger, then I gave him a few sunflower seeds.

Back upstairs, I suddenly realized that in my haste at leaving the DiAngelos', I hadn't put a single thing away. I hadn't even closed up their garage!

I moaned and slapped my hand against my thigh, then called Tilly in and got back on my bicycle.

Right away at the DiAngelos', I sensed something wasn't right. As I walked down the hill to the boathouse, I heard a noise, like a door closing, and froze, midstep. My eyes darted around. I didn't see anyone, but I noticed that the garbage bag I had filled with brush and trash had been spilled out.

Forcing my feet to move, I made my way toward the boathouse and saw that the trash was strewn everywhere, like it had been kicked around. And that the rake I had dropped when I found the drill now leaned up against the building.

Cautiously, I opened the door to the boathouse. "Who's here?" I called in.

At first, silence. But then, a soft scraping noise confirmed my suspicion, and Digger slowly stood up from where he'd crouched behind a grain barrel in the corner. Because of the way the light came through the boathouse, he was a silhouette, but I knew the compact, lean body and the way he held his muscular shoulders back.

"What are you doing here?" I demanded.

"You know darn well what I'm doin' here, Brady."

"You're looking for the drill," I said.

Digger stepped around the barrel. "And if you know what's good for you, you'll give it to me."

"It's not here."

"Well, then. If you picked it up, it's got your fingerprints on it, too, doesn't it?"

I scowled. "I had my work gloves on," I said, but the truth is that I had taken my gloves off before I picked up the drill. It never occurred to me then that I might be handling evidence!

Digger's voice started to sound panicky. "I'm tellin' you, Brady, if you don't get rid of that drill and keep your mouth shut, you'll be in a lot of trouble."

"You *did* do it, didn't you? You put holes in Mr. DiAngelo's kayak."

Digger didn't say anything, but I took the silence to mean yes.

"You and J.T.?" I pressed.

Digger's mouth became a tight, straight line. "You couldn't never prove it!"

An image of the red kayak, lying on the bottom of the river, flashed through my mind.

"Why?" I threw up my hands. "Why'd you guys do it?"

Digger looked away for a second, and when he looked back at me, his voice had lost its angry timbre. "You remember that day we went over there in your boat, Brady? The day we had us a smoke?"

I settled my hands back down on my hips, recalling an

afternoon in early April when Digger said he had something to show us—and the "something" turned out to be a cigarette.

"Yeah," I said, frowning. "I remember."

"Well, think back on it," Digger told me.

So I did. I thought back to how we had gone there, to the DiAngelos' beach, because it was a favorite spot of ours. We hadn't been worried about the new property owners seeing us because their new house was out of sight, up the hill beyond their new, three-car garage.

Nearby, Mr. DiAngelo's new, red kayak rested on two wooden sawhorses. We'd already seen the kayak. We three just happened to be at the 7-Eleven a few weeks previous when Mr. DiAngelo pulled into the parking lot with the new kayak strapped to the top of his silver Porsche. It was quite a sight because the kayak was longer than the car. Agape, we'd stood on the sidewalk with our sodas while he waved and dashed into the store.

"Probably needs to run in and buy a Rolex," J.T. had joked.

"Yeah, or a diamond stud to put where the sun don't shine," Digger had muttered.

The kayak rested on the sawhorses by the DiAngelos' dock, the day Digger tried to get us to smoke.

"Come on, what are you afraid of?" Digger had goaded me, shoving the cigarette in my face.

"I had an uncle who died from lung cancer," I'd told him. Carl's dad, in fact, and I didn't want anything whatsoever to do with smoking.

Digger had cupped his hands around the cigarette to relight it after the wind put it out. Then he blew smoke out the side of his mouth like an old pro and offered it to me again. "One puff ain't gonna turn you into an addict."

I had to screw up my face to make the point. "They make me gag."

So Digger had turned to J.T., thrusting it at him. "For cryin' out loud, you weakling, it's not like you're gonna keel over and die right here on the spot."

Digger had a way of pushing J.T. around, and darned if J.T. didn't accept that cigarette, take a quick puff, and hand it back.

It was at that moment that Mr. DiAngelo had shown up with a golf club in his hand. Scared the you-know-what out of us. He must have been behind the house, practicing his swing or something, and heard us talking.

"What are you guys doing?" he'd asked.

J.T. was coughing, but we'd both stepped away from Digger, who brought the cigarette down quickly and pulled his incriminating hand behind his back.

"I see," Mr. DiAngelo had said. "Look, it's none of my business if you guys are smoking. But it *is* my business when you're on my property. You guys need to leave. I catch you here again, I'm calling your parents."

I had hung my head I was so ashamed. It was only a couple weeks before that I'd baby-sat for Ben all afternoon.

"That's it. Out of here!" he had ordered us.

"I'm sorry, sir." I had tried to apologize. "We didn't mean anything."

Mr. DiAngelo had spun away. He didn't even wait to make sure we were gone.

We did leave, though. Got right in my boat and went home. I was *so* ticked off at Digger I could barely stand to look at him.

When we got back to the dock at my house, Digger was itchy for revenge. "Let's do somethin' to get back at that creep." (Except he didn't say "creep.")

I had waved a hand at him. "I've got homework. I'm going in."

"You, then," Digger had ordered J.T. "You owe me one for the other day when Curtis was hittin' on you."

Curtis was an incredible bully at school.

They had set off down our driveway, arguing, while I went inside.

I had never looked back at them. And it had never, *ever* occurred to me that they didn't blow off their steam and go home that day! That instead, they went down to my dad's workshop, stole the drill and the glue, and sneaked back to the DiAngelos' beach.

I squeezed my eyes shut recalling these events. When I opened them again, I looked sadly at Digger. "You did it because Mr. DiAngelo kicked us off his property?"

"He didn't need to talk to us the way he did," Digger argued. "But you know damn well, Brady, it goes a lot deeper than that. I hate DiAngelo! How the hell did I know his wife was gonna take the kid out for a spin in that kayak?"

I shook my head, not wanting to believe what I was hearing.

"Look, Brady," Digger pleaded as he came up to me, "no one knows what happened. If you get rid of the drill and don't say anything, no one will *ever* know—and none of us will get in trouble."

"But, Digger, it was *wrong*, man. I mean, Ben's dead!"

Suddenly Digger grabbed the front of my shirt. "You think tellin' the cops is going to change any of that? You think tellin' the truth brings the kid back?"

I knocked his hand off and pushed him away.

"No!" Digger came back at me so angrily he practically spit in my face. "It just makes it worse! Because then they'll accuse us of murder!"

"Murder?" I repeated in disbelief. I stared at him.

"Yeah! *Murder!* They'll send us all to reform school—J.T., me, and *you, too,*" he railed, thumping me on the chest with his finger. "Because don't you forget, Brady—it was your frickin' idea in the first place!"

CHAPTER SIXTEEN

My mother's cool, gentle hand on my forehead was like an ice cube on a bonfire, I thought. She had no idea the torment that ravaged me inside, even though I was stretched out, quiet and still, on the living-room couch, Tilly on the floor beside me.

"You don't look so good, Brady. What's wrong?"

"My stomach," I told her. The last thing I wanted to do was go to a Memorial Day picnic with my parents.

"Your stomach," she repeated. "What did you eat for lunch?"

"Chicken," I mumbled. "Mrs. DiAngelo left me some chicken."

Mom sucked in her breath. "Chicken! I'll bet that was it. You've got to be so *careful* with chicken."

"I'll be all right," I argued. "It's just a stomachache. You and Dad go on ahead."

"You're sure?" she asked with a pained expression. "I made that lemon cake you like—"

"Mom, *please*—the last thing I want to do is eat."

She dropped her hands in her lap and nodded sympathetically. "Well, can I get you something before I go? A ginger ale? An ice water?"

I barely moved my head. "Nothing."

After my father was done showering, they dragged a cooler across the floor in the kitchen, dumped in a bunch of ice, and packed up stuff. It took them so long I thought they'd never leave. But finally Dad came to the doorway and said, "We won't be late. If you feel better and change your mind, call us at Uncle Henry's."

"Okay," I replied, keeping the back of my hand over my eyes.

As soon as I heard the door latch, I stood up and went to the kitchen window to watch them drive away. I bit my thumbnail and then I actually cried a little because *I did not know what to do.*

I sank back down in a kitchen chair, then leaned forward and held my head in my hands. The right thing was to go to the police and tell them what happened. It was so obvious. But then I started thinking about how much trouble we'd all be in. What if Digger was right about the murder charge? About us all being to blame? Even if I didn't take part in drilling the holes, it *was* my idea . . .

Reform school would be awful. And it would just *kill* my parents. They wouldn't be able to face any of the neighbors again. They might even want to move! But how could they?

Dad's work is here, on the river, in the workshop. We loved it here. This was home!

I stood up and started to pace the room.

If I said something, if we all ended up in trouble, then J.T. and Digger might never, *ever* talk to me again. I knew how much it had hurt the past month, them shutting me out. Imagine what it would be like forever! Not only that, but all the kids at school would think I was a snitch if I told on my two best friends. Even if *I* got in trouble, too! I would have to go to school someplace else—Mom and Dad would have to get permission for me to go to high school in Kent County or something.

I stopped walking and slapped a hand on my forehead. Tilly whined. My pacing had confused her. I knelt and scratched behind her ears for a minute, and while I did, I looked into her soulful brown eyes, wishing she could tell me what to do.

"Come on, let's go outside," I told her.

We walked down to the water, and for a long time I sat cross-legged at the end of the dock while Tilly sniffed around in the marsh. The soles of my shoes were still caked with chicken manure, but I didn't care. I pulled my Swiss army knife out of my pocket and must have opened and closed it a hundred times. But I couldn't seem to come up with a decision about what to do with the drill. Turn it in? Keep it hidden? Get rid of it? What?

Maybe *no* decision *was* my decision, I thought.

I closed up the knife and slid it back in my pocket.

When Mom and Dad came home at ten-thirty, I met them in the kitchen and told them I was feeling better, even though I wasn't really.

"Thank goodness," Mom said, cutting me a thick slice of leftover lemon cake. "I worried you had food poisoning."

I sat at the kitchen table eating the cake with a glass of milk, but I couldn't finish.

"Why don't you get some sleep?" Mom said. "It's been a long day."

Boy, she had no idea just how long it *had* been.

"I will," I said. But after my parents went to bed, I stayed at the kitchen table. A moth had come in the door and was trying to beat itself to death on the light over the kitchen sink. It got to me after a while, although it sure was entertaining Tilly, who sat at attention and monitored its every move. Between the annoying smack and flutter, and the lump of cake that sat in my stomach, I felt I had to do something. So I finally did go to bed. Even though I knew I couldn't sleep.

Mrs. DiAngelo returned a couple days later, but she came home alone and she didn't seem happier. She had those dark pockets under her eyes again, like she hadn't slept either, and her hair was pulled into a skinny ponytail that didn't look clean. I knew I couldn't ask, but I wondered what had happened with her husband. And I wondered if he still blamed her for Ben dying.

"Did you see the boathouse yet?" I inquired gingerly.

Mrs. DiAngelo sat at the table in her bathrobe, halfheartedly trying to make a list of chores for me, but she perked up a little when I asked.

"No, I haven't," she replied, looking up at me.

I found myself watching her, but every time she moved her eyes toward mine, I focused on something else.

"Show me!" she said, putting down the pencil and grabbing her coffee.

We walked down the hill to the boathouse together. Over the past two days I had cleaned out the entire place and had eighteen leaf bags tied up ready for the trash, along with two big piles of junk: one about five feet high for the landfill, and one with some decent stuff including a porch swing and a twin-size bed frame for the Salvation Army.

"Good job!" she complimented me. "I can't believe you did all this!"

"My dad's got a pickup truck," I told her. "He said we could come get this stuff one evening when he's done work and haul it out of here for you."

"That would be great." She really seemed amazed. "You must have worked like a dog, Brady!"

"It *was* hot," I conceded, staring at my shoes.

"Well, I think a bonus is in order—"

"No!" I protested.

She looked at me funny. Maybe because I had practically shouted at her.

"I'm going to insist," she countered, folding her arms. "Brady, if you work for me, you get paid."

I didn't want to fight her, and I didn't want to make a big thing out of it. "Just regular hours," I agreed weakly. "*Please.* Nothing extra."

Honestly, the money meant nothing to me. And I was beginning to wonder about something else.

While she was turned away, examining an old peach basket I'd put in the throwaway pile, I sucked in my breath. When she turned around, I warned her. "I don't think I'll be able to work for you—"

"Brady! But why?"

Her disappointment surprised me, made me sink back. I licked my lips, bit them. I couldn't bear to add to her problems.

"Not for a while anyway," I replied. "See, I've, ah . . . got exams this week, and I need to study—"

"Oh, exams. Sure, I understand."

I had to think fast because that only bought me a few days.

"You scared me," Mrs. DiAngelo said. "I'm not sure I'd know what to do here without you."

"But that's just it, see. Because after school's out, I'm going up to Rhode Island—to visit my cousins." I said this even though I wasn't sure Mom had actually made those arrangements.

"Oh—"

"It was planned a long time ago," I added, sounding apologetic.

"It's okay, Brady," she assured me, smiling and patting me on the arm so I wouldn't feel bad about leaving her. "That's important, too."

I sighed, feeling a little relieved. It gave me two weeks. Exams. A trip to Rhode Island. Two weeks and time away from her. Time away from *everybody*, I thought. Maybe that's what I needed.

Or was I just running away?

CHAPTER SEVENTEEN

Hey there, stranger!" Carl called out.

I hadn't seen Carl for a while, but he came that morning to pick me up in the ambulance because it was the last day of school.

"How's it going?" he asked as I opened the passenger door. "You been stayin' out of trouble?"

I stepped up into the vehicle and slid onto the seat. "Yeah. Final exams will do that for you." I tried to laugh as I pulled the heavy door shut, but his question wasn't funny. I was in a heap more trouble than I'd ever been in my whole life.

Carl started off down the driveway. "How's the job going for Mrs. DiAngelo?"

"Okay. I'm not working this week because of exams, but I've been mowing the grass and stuff."

Carl was kind of quiet for a few seconds, and I hoped he didn't think it was weird, me working for her after what had happened. I'd been worried about how people would see it,

I guess. Especially kids at school. I looked over at him, but I couldn't see his eyes because of his dark glasss.

"I'm making *really* good money," I pointed out. "Dad even said it was good I had another job this summer because crabs are few and far between."

Carl came back to life. "Yeah, I hear the season started out pretty slow."

As we rode along, I wondered if I should tell Carl about the drill. I even imagined us pulling up behind the Dumpster at the 7-Eleven for a few minutes so I could fill him in on what had happened. He'd listen, I knew he would. Then I could ask him what he thought I ought to do.

I bit hard on the inside of my cheek. It still scared me to think of anyone else finding out.

"How'd you do on those exams?" Carl asked, breaking into my thoughts.

"All right, I guess." I was pretty sure I'd done okay, although not as well as I could have. "I had a hard time concentrating," I said. "I don't know why." A lie because I knew darn well what was on my mind. All week long, every time I saw J.T. or Digger, we avoided one another—until the day Digger caught up with me after school when I was cutting across the field by the tennis courts. I'd been heading for the post office, where Mom was picking me up. She did that sometimes, to avoid all the traffic in the parking lot when school let out.

"Brady, hold up!" Digger had called. "I been lookin' for you all day."

I had waited for him to catch up.

Nervous and fidgety, Digger had stood there, rubbing his hands together. "Look, I just wondered what you ended up doin' . . . you know, with that drill."

Just like Digger to get right to the point.

"Nothing," I'd told him.

"Nothin'? What do you mean, nothin'?"

"Just what I said, Digger. I didn't do anything with it. It's at home."

He had leaned toward me. "What? Are you *crazy*?"

"Hidden—it's hidden, okay?"

Digger had rolled his eyes dramatically and shook his head. "Geez, you can't take the chance, Brady! You gotta get rid of it!"

"Yeah, yeah," I'd mumbled, turning away.

"Come on, it's for the best!" Digger had called after me. "Just *do it*, Brady! Then everyone will forget what happened."

That's what stopped me. The bit about everyone forgetting because I knew no one would. Never in our lifetimes would anyone ever forget what had happened. I swung right around without missing a step and walked straight back to him. Must have looked pretty angry, too, because Digger stepped back and balled up his fists, lifting them up above his waist, like I was getting ready to take a punch at him.

"Let me put it this way," I'd said point-blank. "What if it was Hank, or LeeAnn, your little sister, in that kayak, Digger? Huh? What if Hank or LeeAnn froze to death in the river that day? You think *you* could just walk away and say everybody would forget about it?"

A cruel thing to say because I knew how much Digger loved those kids. He was always looking out for them. *Always.* But I had to make him see.

Digger was speechless. Slowly, he brought his hands down.

Turning, I stomped away again, all the way across the field to the post office. But opening the door to Mom's car, I glanced over the roof and saw that Digger was still standing there in the field.

I stared out the window of the ambulance thinking back on this just as we came up on Digger's house. Carl slowed down because there was a police car in the yard. Thoughts scrambled in my head. Did the truth get out? I sat up and a muscle tightened in my chest.

"Big fight there early this morning," Carl said, stopping.

"Here? At Digger's?"

"Yeah."

My eyes widened; I wondered if Digger's father had let him have it, if he found out the trouble Digger was in and flew off the handle.

"Same old thing," Carl said. "The old man beatin' up on his wife."

Carl knew all this stuff because he listens to the police radio, plus a lot of those police and firemen hung out together. "I hear she took the kids over to her sister's, in Denton," he said.

"Digger's mom always does that," I told him. "Every time they have a fight, she takes the kids and leaves. Then, two days later, she comes back."

We stared at the mess in Digger's front yard: tires, rusted wheel rims, an old automobile frame up on cinder blocks, a large wooden spool from some wire Digger's father had hauled once.

I turned to Carl, hesitating a little before I asked, "Do you know what the fight was about?"

Carl shook his head. "Nah. Probably wasn't nothing *to* fight about! It's just him—Old Man Griswald, drinkin' and bein' ornery." He shook his head. "Digger's mother ought to have that guy arrested."

I sighed with relief, then looked back at Digger's house. Even if I was mad at Digger for what he'd done, I couldn't help but feel a little bit sorry for my old friend. "Digger's mom is too afraid to do anything," I said. "I remember once, Digger told me how his parents had such a big fight in the middle of the night that he took his little brother and sister and walked over to his grandfather's house. I always thought that was so sad, Digger and those little kids padding down the road dead of night, in their slippers. And to get away from their own parents!"

"A real shame," Carl said. He shifted out of park and drove on. "I'm sure Digger won't be in school today."

"No—I guess he won't," I agreed, realizing at the same time that Digger would miss the ceremony this afternoon, the one where we graduated from middle school.

At 2 P.M., the entire school shuffled into the auditorium, where each of us eighth graders was awarded a certificate and a discount coupon to Kings Dominion, an amusement park down in Virginia. A few kids got some awards. Most Musical. Most Athletic. That kind of thing. I stood twice for recognition—once, with the kids who were on the honor roll all three years, and second, because I played on the Sea Hawks' tournament-winning basketball team.

Half a dozen parents came to watch, but most of our parents had to work, including my own. After the sixth and seventh graders went back to class, we stayed for refreshments. A couple mothers had a table spread out with plates and napkins and a big white bakery cake that had *Congratulations* written on it. It looked nice, but that type of cake is way too sweet for me. I didn't even take a piece, just picked up a paper cup full of lukewarm green punch and sipped at it.

Afterward, while I was kneeling down to clean out my locker, I was surprised to hear J.T.'s voice.

"Brady," he said.

Despite everything, I was glad to see him. "Hey," I said, standing up.

"How's it goin'?" J.T. asked.

"Okay," I replied, scratching the back of my neck. I wondered if he was going to ask about the drill, too. "How about you?"

J.T. shrugged. "My dad's still sick."

"That's too bad," I sympathized.

"So I've been working a lot."

A long moment followed when neither one of us said anything. I reached into my locker and peeled off the class schedule taped inside the door.

"I just wanted to thank you," J.T. said.

I frowned. "For what?"

"You know." He glanced around suspiciously then lowered his voice to a whisper. "For not saying anything."

What were we now? A bunch of criminals? I crumpled the schedule in my hand.

J.T. seemed anxious. He kept licking his lips. "So—maybe—you want to come over tomorrow?"

"I can't. I'm going up to Rhode Island to see my cousins." As I said that, I wondered if he'd think I was lying because of how he made up a story about seeing his cousins right after Ben died.

J.T. hung his head. "Brady, I just wondered if we could . . . you know, like, be friends again."

We allowed our eyes to meet. Of course I wanted to be friends. More than anything else in the world I wanted us to be friends. I didn't want anything to change in my life *or* his! But it didn't mean I wasn't angry at him for what he did with Digger.

J.T. shrugged. "I just want us to be friends, that's all."

"Yeah. Sure," I replied softly.

"Is that a yes or a definite maybe?" J.T. asked, his voice lifting a little.

A *definite maybe* was an oxymoron. The slightest glimmer in his eye caught mine before he raised his hand. "Have a good time in Rhode Island—call me when you get back," he said, curling the fingers in his hand and cuffing me lightly on the shoulder.

CHAPTER EIGHTEEN

The airfare to Providence, Rhode Island, was too expensive without reserving a seat way ahead of time, so my mom purchased an Amtrak ticket on-line and took me to the train station in Baltimore early the next morning.

It was a two-hour drive to Baltimore from where we lived on the Eastern Shore. When we arrived, Mom bought us coffee lattes and a huge, gooey Cinnabon, which we shared with two plastic forks while we waited on a wooden bench.

"This trip will be good for you. I just hope you're careful," Mom said.

"I'll be all right," I promised. Honestly, I looked forward to the eight-hour trip by myself. I had a backpack full of stuff just for the train: my CD player, snacks, a book to read. Plus a lot to think about.

"In New York City, just *stay* on the train. Even though it stops, don't get off," she reminded me.

I regarded her coolly. "Mom, I *know*. I'll be *fine*," I insisted, lifting the cup of latte and blowing at the steam. When

I looked at her again, she was gazing at something on the ground, and I noticed for the first time how tiny lines had clustered around her eyes. Had they always been there? Or was she worried? Had the past month been hard on her, too?

Gently, I asked, "What will you and Dad do while I'm gone?"

She looked up and started to smile. "Work in the garden probably. And your father needs shoes. We might take a ride over to the mall one day."

The mall was in Annapolis, over the Bay Bridge, ninety minutes from Bailey's Wharf. I was a little sad they'd be going without me. I speared the last big bite of Cinnabon and started cutting it in half with the edge of the fork.

"Brady," Mom said, her voice changing, "I'm worried about you and your friends."

I stopped cutting. "What do you mean?"

"I don't know." She crinkled up her eyes. "You boys never see each other anymore."

I nodded, agreeing, and wondered if my mother had further suspicions.

"Is it because of what happened with Ben?" she asked.

I hesitated, but then I said, "Yeah."

Mom waited for me to say something more, but I didn't.

"Unfortunately," she began, "sometimes people just don't know what to say when there's been a tragedy. Maybe J.T. and Digger feel like they need to give you some space for a while."

I studied her as she spoke and decided she didn't suspect anything more.

"You're right," I told her. "I think that's all it is."

Just then my train was announced, and I practically jumped up, flustered, eager to escape, the Cinnabon container still in my hands.

Mom stood with me and brushed some crumbs off my shirt. "Why don't you have the boys over when you get home?"

"Good idea," I agreed quickly, handing her the pastry. "Here, Mom—you can have the rest."

She set the box down and gave me a hug good-bye.

I was lucky when I climbed aboard and found a window seat because the train was pretty full. A real mix, it seemed, of people with loud, noisy kids on vacation, and quiet, well-dressed business types. Quickly, I stashed my duffel bag in the overhead compartment. The man I would sit beside had his laptop open and his *New York Times* folded up and stuffed into the side of his seat. He had to pick everything up and turn sideways for me to get by, but he was nice about it.

When the train started moving, he went back to work, tapping away on his laptop. I pushed my backpack up against the seat in front of me and got comfortable, then watched all the dumpy backyards and trash-filled alleys slide by as we pulled out of Baltimore.

For a long time, I stared out the window until I realized that the city had slipped away. I leaned forward to unzip my backpack and rifled around inside until I found my CD player. I knew I needed to make a decision on this trip about what to do with that drill, but I didn't want to start thinking about it yet, so I put some music on, adjusted the earphones, and settled in for the ride.

Up ahead, the train, like a snake, was making a gradual right turn, granting me a clear view of the engine and the cars in front of mine. It reminded me of the steam train ride my parents took me on years ago. The trip was a birthday present when I turned nine, and J.T. and Digger had come along. The train ran out in western Maryland, which is pretty far away, so we drove out late one afternoon and spent the night at a Holiday Inn. The next day, we boarded the train in Cumberland and rode up a mountain to Frostburg and back.

We all got cinders in our eyes—but we had a blast on that train ride. Just thinking of it again made me realize how, growing up, we three were together all the time: camping out, exploring the woods, shooting baskets, fishing. We loved playing pirates, too, and talked all the time about how we'd grow up to be Navy SEALs. My dad even helped us make our own boat once.

Boy, we loved that little dinghy we made. We'd row it all the way down the Corsica River to Pioneer Point, where the Russian embassy in Washington, D.C., has a summer place. The Russians had buoys out in the river for their boats and we'd row up, quiet as we could, beside them, then suddenly sing the national anthem—REAL LOUD—because everybody said those buoys were bugged.

We sure did have us a time, I was thinking, and it was pretty neat, sharing a dream with J.T. and Digger. But there's no way I'll ever end up a Navy SEAL. This'll sound crazy, I know—a kid like me from the boonies on the Eastern Shore—but what I want to do someday is design buildings—maybe even parks and stuff. At home, on the shelf next to my basketball trophies, I have a whole city of cardboard buildings that I carved out with my X-Acto knife.

J.T. (his real name is Jeremy Tyler) is not likely to become a Navy SEAL either. His father probably wants him to take over the family business one day. It's only the biggest chicken farm in the county with flocks of fifty thousand birds at a time. But the thing is, J.T.'s a total computer geek—or *genius*, depending on the way you want to look at it. I remember how one Friday, J.T., Dad, and I took a shopping list over to Computer Renaissance in Annapolis, bought the parts, and J.T. put together a computer for us that weekend. DVD driver, CD burner, the works. J.T.'s future is definitely cyber, not chicken.

Just then the train crossed a wide body of water, which I figured to be the Susquehanna River. We'd be crossing into Delaware next, I figured.

But Digger? Would Digger become a SEAL? I thought about that. Maybe. Maybe one day he would. Either that or a Marine. He loves everything about the Marines—right down to the food they eat. J.T. and I—we'll pig out on Bagel Bites and frozen cheese pizza—and we can put away a whole bag of spicy nacho chips between us. But Digger would turn all that good food down in a heartbeat for a pack of MRE rations. MRE, as in Meals Ready to Eat. Military food that comes in slick, brown plastic bags. His mother picks them up for him every once in a while at the army surplus store when she's in Annapolis. Digger made me try one once. We sat in the cab of his dad's dump truck and tore open the bags: beef stew, applesauce, shrink-wrapped crackers, little packets of strawberry jam, iced-tea mix, and hot chocolate. There were matches, too—for cigarettes? Plus two pieces of Chiclets chewing gum and one of those moist towelette things for wiping your hands off.

Digger might as well become a Marine. He already looks like one with his buzz haircut. And you ought to see him in his hunting clothes grunting away, doing pull-ups on that rusted swing set in his backyard. My mother used to say if he applied himself, he could get into the naval academy. But I doubt it with the kind of grades he makes.

His real name is Michael. Michael Griswald. But when he was little, he loved the backhoe so much they called him Digger, and it stuck. Funny, how we all had nicknames. Even my dog, Tilly, which is short for Tighlman Island, where she came from.

My mind sure was drifting. Looking back, I could see there were things we three did that I would never forget. Boy, like the day we were playing ice hockey and I went through the ice on that cow pond. It was Digger who saved my life. I can still see him sprawled toward me, his chin bleeding, his tooth chipped forever, reaching both of his bare, cold hands out to me while I thrashed around in that freezing water and couldn't get a grip because the edges of the ice kept breaking. *"Grab on, Brady! Grab on!"* And J.T. in the background, holding Digger's ankles so he wouldn't go down with me.

Suddenly Ben's little face broke into my mind, scattering all those memories like ice chips. His little face with the blueberry eyes and the big dimples. My hands curled up into fists and my chest got tight remembering something Carl once told me: *Hypothermia makes you shiver real bad, then your muscles get rigid and you kind of go into a stupor and pass out. . . .*

I turned toward the window and bit my lip. God, I hoped Ben didn't suffer. I hoped that however it happened, it was quick. Real quick. So quick he didn't feel anything or even have time to get scared.

Just then, the train's air-conditioning or something must've kicked into overdrive because I felt a chill blow right through me. I shifted position in that train seat and rubbed my arms hard, but for a long time I couldn't get warm and finally had to get up and pull a sweatshirt out of my duffel bag.

CHAPTER NINETEEN

Brady!" my cousin called at the top of his lungs.

I set my bag down and whirled around to see my cousin Kevin, waving on the train platform in North Kingston, Rhode Island. My other cousin Emily jumped up and down beside him, and my aunt stood smiling.

We hadn't seen one another since last summer when we vacationed together at Stone Harbor, New Jersey, and it struck me right away how much taller Kevin was. We were the same age. Did I seem bigger to him? And Emily, who was only seven, had grown, too. Her hair, short and blond at the beach just months ago, was darker—and long enough for a ponytail, which swung behind her head as she ran up to me.

"What did ya bring me?" Kevin asked like a little kid, taking my duffel and grinning. He had a terrific smile—a million freckles on his face—and new wire-rimmed glasses that made him look smart.

"I brought you a piece of gum," I joked. I knew we had

packed something for him, but I couldn't remember what.

My aunt, who looks a lot like my mom only thinner, gave me a hug.

"How was the trip?" she asked.

"Good," I replied.

"Were you scared?" Emily asked.

I shook my head and chuckled. "No, it was fun."

"Ahhhhh. I want to do that, Mom," she whined. "Can I someday? Can I take the train to Maryland by myself?"

"We'll see," Auntie Janet said, using a phrase that was very familiar to me.

It had already been a long day, but it was only five o'clock when we pulled into their driveway in Jamestown. Kevin had to leave right away for a clarinet lesson, so I put my things on the cot set up in his room and let Emily pull me into the basement playroom to see her Barbies.

"Do you want to play?" she asked eagerly.

I sat on a hassock and wrinkled my nose. "I'll just watch, okay?"

It was sort of fun watching Emily. She made me think of my sister, though, because Amanda would have been the same age, only one month younger. I had a hunch my sister would have been a tomboy—like J.T.'s sister Kate. She would have learned how to bait trotlines, pitch a tent, and play basketball. But even so, I thought, sitting there, I wouldn't have minded a bunch of Barbie dolls and stupid girl stuff like that if she could have lived.

When Emily finished dressing one of her Barbies, she held it up.

"Pretty cool," I said, taking the doll in my hands. "What's this in her hand? A pocketbook?"

"No, silly!" Emily exclaimed. "That's her Palm Pilot!"

"A Palm Pilot? Boy, she's lucky. *I* don't even have one of those!"

Emily lifted her chin and snatched the doll back. "That's because she has a job. She runs a company, and she has to stay organized."

"Oh," I said, deciding I'd had enough of Barbie. "Look, I think I'd better go help your mom with dinner."

But upstairs, my aunt didn't need help. She told me to take a soda and go sit in the den. "Turn on the television if you want."

I chose a Sprite from the refrigerator and turned on the TV, but there wasn't much on, so I clicked it off and started browsing through the family photograph albums on the bookshelf beside me. I discovered myself in the first one I opened—a picture of Kevin and me when we were little, sitting in our long johns on the couch. I had to grin, remembering how comfortable those pajamas were. I had a pair once with rocket ships, and another pair with lizards.

The pictures brought back some neat memories. In one photograph, we all had our fishing poles—me and Dad, Uncle Larry, Kevin, and my older cousin Joey, who was away at college now. In another picture, we were gathered around Auntie Janet's kitchen table, celebrating Joey's twelfth birthday with a cake.

Beneath Joey was a picture of Auntie Janet giving Emily a baby bottle. And on the same page, a picture of my mother hugging a smiling baby. Beside it was a photograph of the same baby sitting in one of those little baby seats beside Mom. I didn't recognize the baby, so I glanced at what my aunt had written underneath the first picture: *Dee holding Amanda, three months old.* Dee is my mother. And—but, of course—what other baby would my mother be holding?

Quickly, I searched my memory as I set the book back down on my lap. The baby in the seat was smiling. She wore pink-footed pajamas. And there were dark curls on her head. Warm tears filled my eyes as I took in these details. After I blinked, everything blurred. Still, I didn't stop staring at that photograph because nothing else came to my mind. It was the first picture I'd ever seen of my sister.

My aunt saw what was happening.

"Brady," she said softly as she crossed the room with a spatula in her hands.

I wiped at my eyes with one hand. "Sorry," I apologized. "But it's the first picture I've ever seen of Amanda."

Auntie Janet sighed and sat down beside me.

"I didn't even remember what she looked like," I told her.

"Oh, she was a beautiful baby, Brady." My aunt smiled.

But I couldn't smile back. "How come Mom doesn't have pictures for us?" I asked.

"I'm sure she has pictures. Somewhere," my aunt said. "But you know, it was all so painful for your mother. For your father, too. I think that the only way your mother could deal with the grief was not to have any reminders around."

I looked up, wondering if Auntie Janet knew about the butterfly garden.

"There's a locked trunk in the attic that has Amanda's stuff in it," I said. "It's like Mom and Dad packed her up and put her away. Like they wanted to pretend she never existed."

"Everybody has a different way of dealing with these things," my aunt replied. "You need to try to understand."

I examined the photograph again and this time detected Dad's eyes in her little face. It's hard to explain, but his eyes are dark, like mine. It looked as though both Amanda and I had Dad's curly brown hair, too.

"It doesn't mean *you* can't have a picture of Amanda," my aunt said. "Would you like this one?"

I didn't even have to think about it. I nodded right away.

Carefully, she lifted the plastic page and removed the photograph of Amanda sitting in her little baby seat. "Here," she said. "Put it in a special place, and when you need to see your sister, she'll be there."

I pulled my wallet out from the back pocket of my jeans and opened it. There was a secret place under my ID, where Mom had me keep an emergency ten-dollar bill. I had to fold the photograph on one edge to make it fit, but I made sure the fold didn't touch Amanda.

It was a comfort, knowing I had a picture of my sister, hidden away in my wallet. Later that night, while Kevin was in the bathroom brushing his teeth, I took her out for one more look, then tucked the photo back under the ten-dollar bill and pushed my wallet deep down inside my duffel bag.

Over the next few days, Kevin and I had a lot of fun riding bikes, playing video games, shooting baskets, skateboarding. Jamestown is on an island, and every day, with Emily, we climbed around on the rocks down by the water and found a lot of neat stuff washed up in the shallow tidal pools: minnows, mussels, periwinkles, even some teeny tiny crabs. We all ate lobsters at Duffy's Tavern. And one day we walked around Newport over on the mainland, where I stopped in a gift shop and bought a paperweight with seashells in it for Dad and, for Mom, a refrigerator magnet that was a miniature version of a lighthouse with a little light that blinked.

I wasn't naive. I knew that this whole week had been a planned effort to get my mind off what had happened in the river. It had worked, too, I thought. I was having fun. The food was good. I slept better at night. I started wishing I could just stay in Rhode Island for the whole summer, sleeping on the cot in Kevin's room. But I knew I'd just be hiding out. Postponing what I had to do. Which was to go home and deal with that drill and the whole problem once and for all.

All the way back on the train I kept turning it over and over in my mind how J.T. *never* would have drilled the holes in that kayak if he thought someone was really going to get hurt, let alone killed! J.T. was a good kid. Hardworking. Honest. I kept thinking about all the years he was homeschooled by his mom and all that religion he had pumped into him. If I told and got us all in trouble, it would blow his family right out of the water! I could just see pages of the Bible floating in the air. And at a terrible time, too, with J.T.'s father in the hospital waiting for a new kidney—and them needing J.T. on the farm.

I slumped into my train seat and turned to look out the window with my chin cradled in my hand, thinking back to when J.T. first came to public school. It was in the sixth grade, right after his father first got sick. His mother couldn't handle teaching the kids at home and running the farm, too, so she sent them off on the bus to school. It was hard for J.T. because he's shy and the only two people he knew were Digger and me and we weren't in any of his classes. The only times we saw him at school were at lunch and during basketball practice.

As if that weren't bad enough, there was this bully, Curtis, who started picking on J.T. all the time. Called him "chicken man." Said out loud how he could smell chickenshit when J.T. walked into a room. I don't know why Curtis chose J.T. to pick on. Because he was new? Because he bowed his head in prayer at the cafeteria table, even if it was just an ice-cream sandwich? Because he looked a little dorky with his tall, lanky body? I honestly don't know. But I could tell you this: The person who defended J.T. the most was Digger. He even got suspended once for fighting with Curtis in the boys' room, where he had taken him on for stuffing feathers into J.T.'s locker.

Curtis stopped picking on J.T. after that. Didn't want to mess with Digger, I guess. Digger's tough. Strong, too. I remember how once he scooped up Hank and put him on his shoulders for a ride and then twirled LeeAnn around by her arms in the front yard, the three of them spinning around and around until they all fell down together, laughing.

Pulling my hand away from my chin, I sat up in the seat. I crossed my arms. Digger didn't mean to kill Ben either. Digger was my *friend*. A friend who once pulled me from a frozen cow pond and saved my life.

We were only thirteen years old. We once shared a dream together. Didn't this matter to anyone?

Uncrossing my arms, I felt for my wallet with its secret picture of Amanda, then squeezed my eyes shut, not wanting to even *envision* the pain I would cause my mother if I— or anyone else—told and got us all in trouble.

When the train made a stop, I gazed out the window, watching people hustle away, clutching their briefcases, pulling their rolling suitcases, putting the cell phones up to their ears. None of their lives were as complicated as mine, I thought. I'd swap with any one of them. I even imagined myself getting off and just walking. Kids my age ran away all the time. But I wouldn't have a clue where to go, and I only had about thirteen dollars in my pocket.

It was just a thought. A crazy thought. Because it wasn't in me to run away.

As we pulled away from the station, bright, afternoon sun streamed through the windows, making me squint. I closed the little curtain and leaned my head back against the seat. I didn't even want to listen to music.

By the time we rolled into Baltimore, hours later, I knew what I had to do.

CHAPTER TWENTY

Tilly barked and ran circles around me she was so excited that I had returned. It was good to be home, throwing the ball for my dog, eating what I wanted, having a bathroom all to myself again.

Summer had taken over while I was gone. It was hot as blazes outside—humid, too, and inside our house, all the air conditioners hummed in the windows.

Dad, his shirt soaked with sweat, brought home some of the crabs he'd caught that day for dinner, and Mom steamed them in a big silver kettle on the stove. Ordinarily we'd pick crabs on a picnic table inside the little screened-in porch we have on the back of the house. But it was too hot, so I spread newspapers out over the kitchen table and got the bucket of wooden mallets from the cabinet above the refrigerator. I fixed each of us little bowls of vinegar, melted butter, and Old Bay spice for dipping the crabmeat. Then Mom set out some cucumber-and-onion salad and a steaming plate full of corn on the cob. One of my all-time favorite meals, I have to say. I must have cracked and picked a dozen crabs before I even started getting full.

After eating, I helped Mom do the dishes while Dad got rid of the messy mountain of empty crab shells we'd left on the table. Peach ice cream for dessert. We took bowls of it into the living room to eat, and I gave my parents their souvenirs. Dad seemed pleased when he set his paperweight on the coffee table. "Look ahere. Now I can keep all those bills in one place," he joked. And Mom got right up to go stick the blinking lighthouse magnet on the refrigerator door.

Dad stretched out his long legs, put his arms up behind his head, and yawned.

"How's the crabbing been?" I asked.

"Terrible," he said, letting out such a long sigh that I was a little sorry I'd asked. "Must have thrown back twenty, thirty sponge crabs today. And I'll tell ya, it kills me, it just *kills* me ever' time to think nobody's doin' nothin' to stop that in Virginia."

Sponge crabs—those are the females, with their eggs. Illegal to keep them in Maryland—you know, an effort to help boost the crab population. But not in Virginia, and they own the water near the mouth of the bay. It's always been a source of irritation to my dad.

"Been a lousy season, Brady," Dad said. "Kenny and I are even talkin' 'bout doin' some perch fishin' to offset it some."

"Perch?" I could not envision Dad and Kenny out there fishing perch instead of hauling crabs.

"Yeah," Dad confirmed, but he didn't sound too enthusiastic about it.

"That reminds me," he said, sitting up and letting his hands fall onto his knees. "I need to run down the marina and pick up some bait for tomorrow. You want to come along, Brady?"

I blew the air out of my cheeks and shook my head. "I'm pretty beat, the train and all."

Mom stood up to gather our empty ice-cream bowls. "I'll go with you, Tom," she offered brightly, "if you'll stop at Ida's and let me run in with that dress she's going to take in for me."

As soon as my parents were gone, I sprang into action.

A piece of apple. Part of a carrot. I put the food in the palm of my hand and went downstairs to the basement, where I opened the top of Tiny Tim's cage. After settling the food inside, I let the hamster sniff my fingers. I felt an ache for Ben then. Ben, who should be here on this earth taking care of Tiny Tim. But it was not enough to stop me from what I was about to do.

Underneath the workbench, I pulled out the box of rags and shoved my hand beneath the curtains looking for the drill. When I felt the bag, I grabbed it and pulled it out. With my foot, I pushed the box back underneath and closed the cupboard door.

By then it was close to 8 P.M., and it had cooled off some outside. I headed down to the water, the bag-wrapped drill in my hand, Tilly running on ahead. At the end of the dock, I climbed down the ladder and got into the little dinghy we kept tied there.

A loud crack cut the air. Tilly had found a huge, horse-shoe-crab shell on the creek bank and was chomping away. Quickly, I drew back on the oars so I could escape without her. I didn't want anyone to see what I was about to do, not even my dog.

In the middle of the creek, I brought the oars inside the boat and let the boat drift. A couple bullfrogs were starting to croak in the marsh grass, and every once in a while there was a little *bloop!* when a fish jumped. But I was jittery being out on the water and wished for a split second I'd thought of some other way to do this.

I looked around, but who was there to see me? So I didn't waste a lot of time worrying. I just took the drill out of the bag and tossed it about three feet away.

There was a little splash and it was gone.

Now, unless I opened my mouth, no one would ever know, I thought. Leastways if they did, they couldn't prove it. My friends wouldn't get in trouble, and neither would I. The way I looked at it, I was protecting J.T. and Digger— and my parents as well.

In the dim evening light I watched the ripples from the disturbed water chase one another, some toward me, and some toward the opposite shore, where they disappeared before long into the dark expanse of water.

CHAPTER TWENTY-ONE

I thought I'd wake up feeling relieved the next morning. Like a weight had been taken off my shoulders because of the action I'd finally taken. But it didn't start out that way, and I wondered while I poked at the scrambled eggs Mom had made whether it was something I just had to get used to first, like a new haircut.

It was still really hot, too. Just stepping outside the door was like walking into an oven. I put some ice chips in Tilly's water bowl and fooled around on the computer some, but I didn't exactly race to the phone to tell Mrs. DiAngelo I was home and ready to go back to work.

Mom seemed glad to have me around. "Why don't you rest up for a couple days," she suggested, pausing on her way out the door to work one morning. "And fold that laundry for me, would you?"

I did. I folded the laundry. And I took a whole week off. But I didn't do anything with the time. Sat around the house mainly, watching television and playing solitaire on the computer. I could tell my father was getting pretty frustrated because every evening he'd come in after being on the water all day and ask me what I did. To which I had to say "not much." Which for some reason prompted my mother to start asking about J.T. and Digger.

It was getting to be a vicious cycle, so finally I did call Mrs. DiAngelo and I went back to work. Mom stopped asking about J.T. and Digger. And Dad didn't have to quiz me on what I did all day. Still, things weren't getting a whole lot better. I don't know. I kept waiting, but I wasn't getting used to the decision I'd made. It didn't feel right.

Fourth of July came, and with it, Mr. DiAngelo. I was surprised when I saw his Porsche in the driveway. While I was getting the mower ready, he came out to the garage and shook my hand, but I didn't think he had his heart in it. And although I can't be sure of this, I had the eerie feeling he was watching me all day.

I could barely wait to leave at noon when Mrs. DiAngelo came out to pay me. Her eyes glistened, like she'd been crying, and all the way home on my bike I wondered if Mr. DiAngelo suspected me of something. Paranoid. I think that's the word for how I was feeling.

Both of my parents worked the Fourth of July, so I was the first one home. Alone in the house with Tilly, I practically jumped when the telephone rang. I didn't want to talk to anyone, so I let the answering machine pick up the call, and from two rooms away, I could hear the distinct, gravelly voice of Tink Bosley, head of the local watermen's group: *"Tom, just so's you know. There's a meetin' next Tuesday, Howard's Dock. We're organizin' a protest of them new crab regulations. I tole Dee earlier, but we changed the time. Six 'stead a five. See y'all there. Thanks."*

I wondered what the watermen had planned, and what Dad thought of this. But there was way too much else on my mind, and I couldn't focus on it.

At the picnic that evening, my father won the anchor-throwing contest, his fourth year in a row. Mom soaked up compliments about her blueberry pies, and I stuffed myself on all the good food laid out. But none of my friends showed up. It was strange being at the Rock Hall marina, given all that had happened there almost three months ago. I avoided the dock area, where I'd brought Ben in. As soon as the fireworks were over, we headed home.

In the kitchen, Dad picked up a note from the table, frowned, and rubbed the back of his neck while he read it.

"I forgot to tell you about that earlier," Mom said as she padded back into the kitchen, already changed into a night-gown and slippers. She opened the cupboard and reached for an empty glass. "Tink said the meeting was important. Everybody's got to be there."

Dad groaned and Mom glanced at him as she filled her glass with water.

"I don't think you have a choice, Tom," my mother said.

"It's America," Dad told her. "You always have a choice."

Mom widened her eyes. "Thomas Parks!" she exclaimed. And my mom hardly ever raises her voice at either one of us. "They'll make your life miserable if you don't go along with that protest."

Dad tossed the note back on the table and seemed resigned. "I know."

The next morning, before she left for work, Mom asked me to help her plant two purple coneflowers someone had given her at the nursing home.

It was another hot day with no sign of rain. Cicadas hummed insistently in the trees, and the soil was dry as dust. While I dug two small holes with the trowel, Mom asked me how Mrs. DiAngelo was doing.

"Well, her husband's back."

"No! That's wonderful!" Mom reacted. "Why didn't you tell me? Gina must be thrilled."

"I don't know about *that*," I said. "She didn't seem all that happy yesterday."

"Why not?" Mom asked.

I shrugged. "I don't know. Maybe he still blames her for what happened."

Mom shook her head. "All I can say is that I'm glad you're over there, helping them, Brady. Gina's so sweet, and with a baby coming, I'm sure she appreciates your help."

Gently, I settled the first coneflower in the earth and packed the powdery dirt in around the roots. Mom handed me the other flower to plant.

"Yeah, but I can't keep working for them," I said.

Mom leaned forward, trying to see my face. "Why not, Brady? Did something happen?"

"No," I told her. A Big Lie. An *enormous* lie. Plus I was discovering that I couldn't look my own mother in the eye anymore either. I finished patting the dirt down with my fingers, and while Mom watered the plants, I stood up, wiping my hands off on my jeans. "I just don't want to be there anymore."

I shouldn't have walked away so abruptly after I said that, but I did. Just up and left. Went inside to my room. And I was thinking the whole time that even if I changed my mind about keeping this whole thing quiet and told the truth—to whom would I tell it? My parents? The DiAngelos? The police? Would it be my word against J.T.'s and Digger's? I mean, how could I prove it now that I'd gotten rid of the drill?

Sitting at my desk, I picked up the old Orioles hat, the one I didn't wear anymore because of Ben, and turned it in my hands. I thought of the red kayak, how I'd seen it sunk on the bottom of the river, and stared at the wall in front of me for—I don't know, five, ten minutes. I knew I was teetering on some sort of edge.

My wallet was on the desk in front of me. I put down the hat and opened up the wallet, then reached behind the hidden ten-dollar bill for the picture of Amanda. Unfolding it, I gazed at her smiling little face. "If you were here, what would you say?" I asked my sister. "I know you'd only be seven years old, Amanda, but you'd be smart like your cousin, Emily. You'd have an idea, I know you would."

Sitting there, holding Amanda's picture, I heard a snuffling noise behind me and swung around.

Mom stood in the doorway, a hand to her mouth. It was obvious she'd been listening.

I braced myself for her to fall apart, but the amazing thing is—she didn't. Quietly, she walked in, feeling for the end of my bed to sit on because she didn't want to take her eyes off the picture in my hand.

"Auntie Janet gave me this," I quickly explained, "when I was up there visiting."

Tears had cropped up in her eyes. "I didn't know . . . Brady . . . that you ever wanted a picture."

"Sure, I did," I managed to say before my own voice cracked. "She's the only sister I ever had."

It's embarrassing for me to describe how we both caved in then and just had it out, crying and hugging each other. All those years we had both missed Amanda so much—and yet we never said anything! It still hurts some when I get to thinking on it, but I try not to go there. So let me just say it was one tremendous relief to get it all out that day with my mother.

"It seems silly," I said to Mom at one point. "She's been gone so long."

"No. No, not silly," Mom disagreed. "We can't forget her, Brady. She's part of who we are. She always will be."

She said something else, too. About how she had to stop blaming herself for what happened to Amanda before she could cope with it and move forward. Then she paused. I knew it was hard for her to talk about Amanda. "It was wrong for me to leave and not be here for you and Dad all those months," she said. "I know how badly that must have hurt you, Brady."

"It did," I readily admitted because I wanted her to know.

I even told her how disappointed I was she and Dad didn't let me go to the funeral. And how I could never go back to the National Aquarium because that was where Carl took me the day they buried Amanda.

Mom closed her eyes. "I am so sorry, Brady."

"It's okay," I told her. Man, I couldn't stand seeing my mom so sad. "Hey! I see enough fish around here every day. I don't need to go to the aquarium!"

She started to smile a little, so I did, too.

"Do me a favor?" she asked in a small voice.

"What?"

"Don't quit working for Gina yet."

How could I say no to my mom after what we'd both been through?

"Good," she said, then she took my hand. "Now come with me. I want to show you something."

Puzzled, I let her lead me into the living room, where she let go of my fingers and lifted the top of a crystal candy dish on the fireplace mantel. I knew there wasn't candy in the dish, but Mom reached inside and picked up a little gold key.

"Here," she said.

I opened my hand and she placed the key in my palm.

"What's this?" I asked.

"The key to the trunk up in the attic," she said. "Amanda's trunk. There's a scrapbook in it. Lots of pictures, some with you in them. Some toys you might remember. Anytime you feel the need, Brady, you can go up. You know where the key is now."

I stared at the key, then looked up at my mother. I loved my mom so much, I thought. It would just kill her to know what J.T. and Digger had done, and how it was all my idea. . . .

"Thanks," I said, and I wrapped my arms around her so hard I thought I could never let go.

CHAPTER TWENTY-TWO

It all came to a head a few days later, the evening Carl popped through the doorway twirling his car keys on his thumb. "Hey, Brady! How about a movie?" he asked. "We could grab a couple subs at the 7-Eleven and pick out a sci-fi at the video store."

Sounded pretty good, actually. Mom was busy canning tomatoes, and I didn't see any sign of dinner. "Go ahead," she encouraged me. So I swept my hat off the end of the counter and off we went in Carl's car.

I figured Carl was going to give me grief about not crabbing this summer and all those pots going to waste settin' there by the shed. But he didn't bring it up. He talked about Mindy for a while, how she was taking evening classes down at the community college. Then he told me about a couple of recent calls he had—an old woman calling 911 because she had a leaky faucet and a mother who called for help when her little kid stuffed black-eyed peas up his nose.

When we walked into the video store, I was still laughing.

I was not prepared to run into J.T. But there he was, smack in the middle of the science-fiction aisle. J.T. loved that stuff as much as Carl and me.

"Hey there, stranger!" Carl greeted him. "How's it going?"

J.T. smiled wanly. I saw that he was holding a copy of *The Invisible Man.*

Carefully, we regarded each other. It had been about a month since I'd seen J.T., and he didn't look so great. He needed a haircut, and his eyes were red-rimmed and seemed kind of sunken.

"How's your dad?" I asked.

"Still waiting for a kidney," J.T. replied. "He's on a list."

"I thought you were going to give him one of yours."

"I can't be a donor," he said, looking down. "You got to be eighteen."

All the time I was watching J.T., I noticed how his whole face had an odd pallor to it. Pale, I guess, like he wasn't getting outside. Was he suffering because he didn't know what I'd done with the drill?

I felt sorry for J.T., I really did.

"Things will be all right," I told him, speaking slow. Our eyes connected. "It'll be okay," I repeated.

Carl lived with his mother, my aunt Tracy, but she was at bingo down to the church, so we had their house to ourselves. Carl threw a bag of chips on the kitchen table and poured us tall, icy glasses of soda—him a Coke, and me a Dr Pepper. Then we ate the subs right there, using the waxy white paper they came wrapped in for plates. I had ordered my favorite, a BLT, while Carl consumed a cold-cuts combo with hot peppers and onions. I'll tell you, my cousin has an iron stomach. I watched him eat a grilled nutria once at my uncle Henry's annual game cookout, and I couldn't even taste that thing. If you ask me, those nutria look just like giant rats.

The movie we rented, *Blade Runner*, was an old one. We'd seen it a hundred times, but we took our shoes off, put our feet up on the coffee table in the living room, and enjoyed the heck out of seeing it again. It did bother me, though, how those futuristic replicants with their limited, four-year life spans, desperately wanted to live longer. The whole movie was about getting "more life," and it got to me after a while. I had to leave the room, but I know Carl didn't notice. I told him I had to use the head.

I wondered, as I stared out my aunt Tracy's bathroom window, if what had happened to Ben would hang like a bag of stones on my heart the rest of my life, dragging me down. And I wondered what it was doing to J.T. and Digger.

Later, while he was driving me home, Carl asked if we were going down to the crab feast in Crisfield. His question surprised me because Crisfield is about a three-hour drive away. "I don't think so," I replied. "Why? Why would we?"

"Why *would* you?" He turned and made a face like *duh*. "Because the watermen are plannin' that big protest!"

"In Crisfield?" I asked. "Crisfield's in the middle of nowhere."

"Anybody who's anybody in this state goes to Crisfield for

that crab feast!" Carl explained. "Delegates, state sena-
tors—the governor. All the political pooh-bahs. *And* all
those media people, too—the newspapers, TV. This is a big
issue, Brady!"

"Oh . . ." I was beginning to understand.

"I just hope it doesn't get nasty," Carl said.

"What do you mean? You think somebody might get
violent?"

Carl stayed focused on his driving. "Some of those watermen are pretty ticked off. I suppose anything could happen."

"Geez, Carl. You think Dad should go?"

Carl rolled a toothpick around in his mouth. "I don't
know," he finally said. "It's a tough issue. The new regulations are hitting those guys hard. Crabbing's their livelihood, Brady. Some of them, they don't know anything else."

I felt bad that I'd been so wrapped up in my own troubles
I hadn't even thought about Dad. I knew he had mixed feelings about the new crab regulations because of what he said
the other night when he got that message from Tink Bosley.

When Carl stopped his car in front of our house, I told
him, "Thanks. I had a good time."

He waved me off. "Don't mention it. Let's think about
taking a little camping trip next month, okay? Up to the
Catoctins, maybe?"

"Sure—that would be fun," I said before getting out.

"Hey!" Carl called after me, leaning across the seat so he
could see me through the open window. "Tell your dad to
be careful tomorrow."

———

When I opened the kitchen door to the house, Tilly practically mowed me down she wanted out so bad. I glimpsed the back of Mom—she had her bathrobe on, her hair caught up in a big clip—and heard the clink of dishes in the sink.

"I'm home!" I called in. "Takin' Tilly out."

She turned around and smiled.

I walked into the butterfly garden while Tilly went off to do her business, and spied a big toad making his way down the brick pathway in the moonlight.

Like that toad, my mind was kind of hopping from one thing to another. My concern for Dad and that crab protest. J.T. and *his* dad. Me and the DiAngelos. I wondered what I would do when I quit working for the DiAngelos. I still didn't want to go back out on the water, but I wasn't old enough to work in the hardware store, or down at the 7-Eleven. And worst of all, I still didn't feel right about what I'd done with the drill.

Life just wasn't moving forward the way it was supposed to. Not just for me, either. Because what if Mrs. DiAngelo never got over losing Ben? And what if Mr. DiAngelo never stopped blaming his wife for Ben's death? And how were J.T. and Digger and I going to live our whole lives keeping all this a secret?

Frustrated, I swiped at a daisy and nipped the blossom right off.

Tilly nudged my leg and I knelt down to hug her around the neck. She gave me a bunch of kisses on the face, and I let her. I was thinking that I had to get hold of myself because I still had a lot of good things in my life: Mom and Dad and Tilly, high school and college, my dream of being an architect.

Suddenly a movement in the darkness caught my eye. The toad had hopped up on one of the thick, flat-topped rocks we had set in the garden.

"Tilly, look!" She started to lunge, but I had her by the collar. "Ah, leave him be," I whispered as the toad sat still as a statue on his tiny moonlit stage. The toad's rock belonged to the butterflies. So they could sit in the morning sun and dry the dew off their wings.

Now that Mom and I could talk more about things, about Amanda anyway, I thought of asking her just how the garden helped her. I know she didn't plant it just to keep herself busy, and I remembered that one time Mom told me butterflies symbolized hope. But did she mean hope for *us*? For her and Dad and me? Or hope for Amanda? Did she think Amanda's soul could live on somehow? And if Mom believed that, then what about other kids who died? Like Ben. Could the little butterfly, asleep in our locust tree, drying his wings off on our rock in the morning, symbolize hope for Ben, too?

I'll tell you, I thought about things that night that never *ever* crossed my mind before.

When I shook my head and looked away, I noticed the light was on down in Dad's workshop.

"Come on," I said, clapping to Tilly as I headed toward the barn.

Dad was sweeping the floor when I walked in.

"Hey," he said. "How was the movie?"

"Good. It was fun."

A set of new hatchway doors for someone's boat leaned up against my father's workbench. He must have just finished them because he always cleaned up after he finished a project. Tilly sniffed the pile of sawdust, and Dad shooed her away with the broom.

"Carl asked me if you were going to Crisfield tomorrow," I said.

Dad kept sweeping, and I wasn't sure he heard the question.

"No," he said after a while.

Pushing my hands into my pockets, I studied him. "I guess it was a tough decision, huh?"

"Nah." Dad wrinkled his nose. "Not so tough." He swept his pile onto a dustpan.

There was an old kitchen stool in the workshop. I pulled my hands out of my pockets, hauled the stool over, and sat down. "But aren't the other watermen gonna give you a hard time now?"

"I'm sure they will, Brady," Dad replied as he dumped the contents of the dustpan into a big garbage can.

I was confused, and Dad finally noticed. He leaned the broom against the workbench and brushed off his hands.

"My mother—your grandma Ellen—she used to say to me, 'Tommy, if you know right from wrong, then the answer is always right there, smack in front of you. It's when you get to thinkin' on it that you get in trouble. Because doin' what's right is not always the easiest thing.'

"And there's no doubt," Dad continued, "it would be far easier for me to go along with the other fellers. Drive down to Crisfield tomorrow and hold up a sign. Raise hell with the governor for clampin' down on us. And keep crabbin' these waters till they ain't nothin' left!"

He rested his hands on the edge of the workbench. "But I'll tell you, Brady, it's wrong. It's the wrong thing for the bay. And it's the wrong thing for me."

I stared at my father—astonished. "You're going to give up crabbing?"

"No, not give it up completely. But you said yourself, Brady, we have to respect the bay's balance. Take the long look. Live more sensitively—"

"I was just telling you what that scientist at school said—"

"But you're right! That scientist is right! And I've known it all along."

Then Dad said something that made me stop breathing.

"It's just that sometimes," he said, "even when the right answer is smack in front of you, you got to reach deep inside yourself to act on it. You know what I'm sayin'?"

I nodded, and I swallowed hard, too, because I understood perfectly. Only I was not thinking of saving the blue crab now. I was thinking about Ben. And Ben's parents. I was thinking about reaching inside to do the right thing so they would know the truth. So Mr. DiAngelo knew it wasn't his wife's fault. So Mrs. DiAngelo would stop blaming herself. And so J.T. and Digger and I faced the world and admitted what had really happened.

Dad plopped down noisily in an old chair and put his feet

up on a toolbox. "But I am *not* gonna lose any sleep over it. No sirree. I got more work in this here shop than I know what to do with. One less waterman out there a couple days a week ain't gonna hurt nobody."

He leaned back, putting his hands behind his head. "And I'll tell ya, I won't miss gettin' up at four o'clock in the morning neither!"

"Dad," I said soberly. I got off the stool and stood. "If I were to ask you to do something really strange, but I said it was the most important thing in the whole world to me, would you do it?"

My father kind of chuckled and said, "It depends on whether it was legal or not, I guess."

I had to grin. "It's legal."

"Then—yeah, sure." He brought his arms down and sat up. "If it was really important to you, son."

The grin slid off my face. "Then I need to ask you."

Dad leaned forward, listening.

I hesitated because I knew that once I said something, I could never take it back. And that everything—and everyone—would be changed by it.

But it was the right thing to do. In my heart, I had known it all along.

"I wondered, Dad, if you would hook up the oyster dredger to the *Miss Amanda* and help me haul something out of the river?"

Arching his eyebrows, my father took a long, hard look at me. It was uncanny, but it was almost as though he could read my thoughts. He asked in a quiet voice, "Would it be a red kayak, Brady?"

I did not turn away. "Yes, sir."

Silence for a moment. "Why?" he asked. "Why in the world do you need to do that?"

I couldn't tell him why. Not then.

"It's just something that I have to do," I said firmly.

And Dad accepted that.

To this day I'm not sure why I couldn't have told him the whole truth of it right then. But I've sometimes wondered if it wasn't because deep down inside I still harbored the tiny flickering flame of hope that if we found the red kayak, its hull would be as smooth and intact as the day Mr. DiAngelo brought it home, a glistening shell, a new toy, on top of his silver Porsche.

CHAPTER TWENTY-THREE

We did not waste time. Crack of dawn the next morning we made our way down to the creek, where a thick mist rose above the still, dark waters. A great blue heron squawked at us for making too much noise and, indignant, took off from a nearby bank as we boarded my father's boat.

Miss Amanda's deck was slick with dew. We stepped carefully so's not to slip as we settled the gear on board.

"Easy now. Remember, this ain't no hot rod!" Dad warned, handing me the key.

Hot rod. Only my dad would say something like that.

"I'll be careful!" I called back over my shoulder as I went up front to turn the key in the ignition. Once the engine was running, I adjusted the radar controls on board the boat while my father reached over to the dock and cast off the lines.

"Go ahead!" Dad hollered as he tossed the last line into the boat.

Leaning into the front window, I looked hard to port to be sure I was clearing the last piling as we pulled out.

Dad went to work getting the grapnel hook ready. He didn't think it was necessary to use the oyster dredger. I was glad, because it would have taken most of a day and a half to get the contraption hooked up. Dad said that if the kayak was still there, we could snare it with the grapnel hook, which was actually an extra anchor he kept on board. It had several pointy flukes on it, so if it caught hold, we could wrap the lines around the machine that acts like a high-powered winch to pull in crab pots and hoist it up that way.

I hadn't slept much, but I was alert and pumped full of adrenaline. Finding the kayak and getting the truth out once and for all was my mission. It didn't matter what kids at school thought or *what* happened afterward. It was something I had to do.

The motor hummed as we moved out, the only boat on the creek. Heavy, gray clouds obscured the sunrise, and a few raindrops already warned us it wasn't going to be a beautiful day. But I didn't care. We needed the rain. It was long overdue, I thought, lifting my eyebrows, just as what I was doing was long overdue.

When Dad came forward and took over steering, I went back to sit on the engine box. We entered the Corsica and then went directly to the opposite bank and the opening off the river where I had discovered Ben and where I'd spotted the sunken kayak last April. As soon as I saw the rotten pilings jutting out of the water, the events of last April tumbled forward in my mind and my stomach lurched.

Backing off on the throttle, Dad carefully maneuvered the boat through the narrow channel along the sandbar. Then he threw the boat in neutral and came back toward me.

I stood at the side, staring into the water near the tip of the sandbar. "Right there," I said glumly, pointing and already disappointed. "That's where I saw the kayak last April."

We both leaned over the edge, trying to get a better look. Although it was starting to sprinkle, the water was clear and shallow enough that we could see the sandy bottom. But there was no sign of the kayak, nor any part of it.

The feeling in my stomach got worse. I'd always known there was a good possibility we wouldn't find it.

"You're sure it was here?" Dad asked.

"Positive," I replied. The scowl on my forehead deepened.

"Why didn't you say somethin' about it last spring?" Dad asked.

I shook my head. "I didn't think it mattered then."

My father didn't ask why it mattered now. He walked forward to a second set of gearshifts in the back of the boat and moved her up a few feet. Again, both of us peered into the river. But the water was deeper—and darker, too. We couldn't see a thing. Plus the rain came harder, churning the surface.

"Not the best day to be doin' this," Dad commented.

"Please. Can we look just a little longer?" I begged.

Dad sighed. Then he put a foot up on the railing and studied the water. "Brady, isn't this the old fishin' hole where you and J.T. and Digger used to come? Place was right smart of fish if I 'member correctly."

"It is," I acknowledged. "Remember I told you? We went swimming here, too. On the other side of the sandbar, it drops off big time. Most of that old dock was here then. We could climb up and dive off."

While he listened, Dad rubbed his chin with one hand, the way he does when he's thinking hard on something. "This is where she tried to come in, right?"

"Right," I told him. "She put Ben on that piling—the one right there, but then she got pulled back out by the current."

Dad nodded. "The tides are strong comin' in and out of this channel. Especially in the spring."

"You think the kayak went out with the tide, then?" I asked.

Dad stopped rubbing his chin. He resettled his hat. "Not necessarily. I think what you've got here, Brady, is a littoral drift."

"A literal what? What's that?"

"Lit*to*ral drift," he repeated. "Look." He took his foot down, pointed behind us, and swept his finger back and forth. "Tides comin' in and out this openin' here push the sand up along the edge, creatin' the sandbar. But as the waves come around the corner, you get this swirlin' effect. It creates a backwater eddy—a dimple, if you will. That would be your swimmin' hole. I'd wager a guess that if the kayak sank anywhere near that sandbar, it got sucked into that hole."

"Let's drop the pole and see!"

"Slow down. We've got to move closer to do that, and I don't want to run aground, Brady."

Carefully, we inched the *Miss Amanda* around the sandbar without beaching her until we were directly above the deep water. Dad set out one anchor so we wouldn't drift and run aground, then he fetched the pole we'd brought along and slowly lowered it into the water to feel around down below.

It didn't take long. Dad hit something right off. Something hard and long. We pulled in the pole and threw out the grapnel hook, watching the attached rope spin from its coil on the boat floor.

"Whew! Must be fifteen, twenty feet!" Dad declared. He bounced the hook up and down until he felt it catch hold. "You ready we start haulin' in?"

"I'm ready," I said.

"All right, then, let's go."

Dad wrapped the line around the bar of the machine that pulls in the crab pots and started moving it slowly. It hummed and made a grating noise.

I stood beside my father and waited, holding my breath, until we saw something break through the surface.

It was a grill. Somebody's damned old Weber grill.

"Must have fallen in off the old dock," Dad said.

"Shoot!" I muttered.

After hauling the piece of junk over the side, I kicked it.

"Can we try again, Dad?"

A little puzzled, he shrugged anyway. "Sure."

We heaved the anchor back in. When it landed, Dad pulled up on the line a few times until he felt as though he had hooked something else. Again, the machine did its work. But after a minute or so, it ground to a stop.

"What's wrong?" I asked.

Dad shook his head. "I don't know."

"Is it too heavy?"

"Shouldn't be. But maybe," he said. "If it's the kayak, it could be full of sand."

He tried to get the machine started, but no luck. "Here, grab the line and we'll haul it in," he said.

I stood behind my father, and each of us got hold of the rope. Then, hand over fist, we pulled. It took all the strength each of us had and then some. I was bracing myself to see a dumb tree branch or cement block somebody had tossed in to anchor a buoy come up. So when I saw the tip of that dirty red kayak break the surface, I was ready to cry with relief.

"Look a-there!" Dad exclaimed. "Be damned!"

Finding it this easy, I knew it was meant to be.

The kayak started slipping, though.

"Don't let go!" Dad shouted.

I jammed my feet against the gunnels and pulled as hard as I could.

"Hold on!" he shouted.

With one more tug, Dad was able to reach over the side and catch the opening of the kayak with his hands. I did the same, and the two of us pulled with everything we had.

The kayak weighed a ton because it was full of water and

covered with slimy mud and algae. But we got it up over the rail.

"Watch out!" Dad hollered.

Jumping back, we let it drop heavily inside the boat.

We were whipped from the effort. Dad sat on the engine box while I knelt on the floor. I tried to catch my breath, all the time staring at the kayak, which had landed bottom up, water and sand dripping onto *Miss Amanda*'s deck. A tiny crab fell out and skittered into a corner.

The steady, gentle rain felt good on my face. The other thing that rain did, it gradually washed away the gunk from the underside of the kayak. In slow motion, right before our eyes, little rivulets of rainwater pushed aside the slime until we could see, my dad and I, how three holes had been drilled into the bottom.

Dad didn't say anything at first. He got up, then squatted beside the kayak, touching two of the holes before he looked at me.

He wore a pained expression I'll never forget. "What is this, Brady?" he asked.

I swallowed hard, and with Dad in front of me, one of his hands still resting on the kayak's hull and the rain pouring down, I told him.

I told him everything.

CHAPTER TWENTY-FOUR

Would my father ever forgive me for my role in it?

The question hovered as the story unfolded. When I finally finished, Dad just sat there, staring at the kayak's wounded hull. Briefly, he dropped his head and covered his eyes with one of his thick, callused waterman's hands, and I weakened, wondering in that moment if my father would ever even look at me the way he used to. In my whole life, would this *ever* be behind us?

When he brought his hand down, he turned to me sadly. "We need to tell the police, Brady."

I nodded and bit my bottom lip. "I know."

At home, Mom opened her arms to me. "It's not your fault," she kept saying.

But Dad remained silent, as he had all the way home in the boat. While I'd repeated everything to Mom, he stood with his arms crossed, leaning against the doorway to the living room.

Afterward, however, Dad was the one to call Carl, to find

out who we should talk to at the police department. Carl said not to call *anybody* until he got there. He came over fast and told us *not* to go to the police!

"You need to protect Brady first," Carl insisted.

"He's right," Dad agreed. "We probably need to get a lawyer."

"A lawyer? You think we need a lawyer?" Mom asked, incredulous.

Dad nodded.

"Damn right, Dee," Carl said. "You can't just go to the police. They may try to lock up Brady for being part of this."

My mother put a hand up to her mouth. I was in a heap more trouble than she had realized.

"What do you think it'll cost us?" Dad asked Carl.

I felt even more horrible then. Because I knew my parents didn't have hundreds—or thousands—of dollars to pay for a lawyer. Dad had been saving up for a new truck, and Mom had been setting aside money for college.

Carl shrugged. "I don't have a clue," he said, "but you know it won't be cheap."

Damn, I thought. It had never occurred to me that we'd need to hire a lawyer. I swore to myself that I would work hard to pay my parents back. Even if college had to wait.

Carl recommended an attorney, and more phone calls were made: to the lawyer, and then to Mom's nursing home, telling them she wouldn't be in.

I stared at the table. I knew this was the deal. I knew it wasn't going to be easy. I just had to remember why I was doing it. *Because it was the right thing to do.* And when I remembered that, something deep down inside, something that had been twisted into a tight knot, relaxed just enough so that I could take in a full and solid breath.

The lawyer Carl recommended was named L. Mitchell Anderson. He had an office up in Chestertown, about twenty miles away, so after Carl left, that's where we went that afternoon.

A secretary introduced us to Mr. Anderson, and we all shook hands.

"Come in, come in. Make yourselves comfortable," the lawyer said, like we had stopped in for a social visit.

He was a handsome guy and a lot younger than I expected, in his early thirties, I'd guess. But he was old enough to have a family of his own. Every shelf in his office boasted pictures of his kids: building sand castles at the beach, swinging baseball bats, waving from sailboats. I figured he wouldn't have an ounce of sympathy for what had happened. Not if he had little kids of his own. I hoped I hadn't made a terrible mistake by coming forward. But then I recalled all those framed pictures of Ben in the DiAngelos' house. . . . His parents had loved him, too. And in my head, I heard the hamster's squeaky wheel turning in our basement.

"We 'preciate your takin' us so quickly," Dad said.

"No problem," Mr. Anderson replied. He indicated for us to take a seat. His nice leather furniture squeaked when we sat down. He offered us all something cold to drink, too, but none of us took him up on it.

"Guess you know basically why we're here," Dad began.

Mr. Anderson nodded. "Yes," he said, turning to me, "but I'd like Brady to tell me the whole story."

So, sitting on that slippery couch between Mom and Dad, I went over it all again, including how it was me who, months before, had suggested we put holes in Mr. DiAngelo's canoe, which gave my friends the idea to steal Dad's cordless drill and sabotage the kayak.

"But maybe we shouldn't tell the police about it being Brady's idea," my mother said, opening her hands. It was the only time she interrupted.

Mr. Anderson held up a finger. "It's important for Brady to tell me everything."

Mom sat back, although I saw her wince when I described tossing the drill into the creek.

"I knew I was destroying evidence," I confessed.

Mr. Anderson leaned back in his big swivel chair. While I talked, he didn't say a thing, or ask any questions, just took notes on a yellow legal pad he had propped up on his leg. When I had finished telling him how Dad and I dredged up the kayak that morning in the rain, he let his chair spring forward and sat, pressing his fingers into a tent in front of his chin.

"Let's look at this piece by piece," he said. "First off, don't be concerned about destroying evidence. They would never have gotten fingerprints off the drill, not after that length of time and with it being exposed to the elements."

He made eye contact with Mom and then Dad. "And don't worry about Brady. Nothing is going to happen to your son."

Mom put a hand on her heart and glanced over at Dad.

Mr. Anderson took off his glasses. "Just coming up with the idea isn't enough to convict someone," he explained. "It could be considered conspiracy, I guess, but even conspiracy has to include a first step, and that has to include some action, not just *talking* about a crime."

"Thank God," Mom murmured.

"Just to be sure," Mr. Anderson continued, "I think we should proffer this information in exchange for the state's attorney's agreement for immunity from prosecution. I'm sure they'll accept it—they don't have a case without Brady."

So it looked as though I wasn't going to get in trouble after all. Still, it was not a jubilant moment. Because even if I was never legally punished, I would have to live the rest of my life knowing Ben was dead and that I was partly responsible—along with my friends, who would really be in for it once I finished telling the police what had happened.

"You look puzzled, Brady," Mr. Anderson observed.

"No, sir," I said. "Just worried. Worried about what's going to happen to my friends, to Digger and J.T."

"The judge will make that decision," he said. "There won't be a trial by jury. No juries in juvenile court."

He put his legal pad up on the desk, and we looked at one another. "It's pretty serious, though. My guess is that your friends will be charged with manslaughter—maybe even second-degree murder."

From the corner of my eye, I saw Mom react by putting her hands up to her face.

I swallowed hard.

"Which one is worse?" I asked timidly, almost not wanting to know.

"Well. Obviously, manslaughter is the lesser of the two evils," Mr. Anderson said. "The law defines manslaughter as killing someone, but without malice aforethought, which means you didn't intend to harm anyone. Like an automobile accident where someone gets killed.

"Second-degree murder, on the other hand, means you *did* intend harm, and even if you didn't mean to kill someone, a death resulted."

"Will they go to reform school?" I asked.

"They don't call it that anymore," Mr. Anderson said. "But if they're convicted, they would serve time in a juvenile facility somewhere."

"How long?" I asked.

He shrugged. "Theoretically, the state of Maryland has custody until they're twenty-one years old."

"Twenty-one?" Honestly, I was not sure that I heard right. The lawyer reaffirmed my question with a nod.

Twenty-one years old?

Mr. Anderson was gathering up his papers. Dad was standing up.

I'd be through with school by the time I was twenty-one. Maybe even out of college . . .

Vaguely, I was aware of Mom's hand on my back.

From there, we went to the police station, where I was told to step into a small, stark room that had nothing but a table, a couple chairs, and a computer in it. Dad, Mom, Mr.

Anderson, a policewoman, and one detective came in after me, and once again I told my story. I was getting worn down by telling it over and over, but I plodded through it, the detective prodding me with questions: *When did you find the drill? What did your friend Digger say when you confronted him? Who was the other boy?*

The policewoman sucked on a butterscotch Life Saver—I could smell it—and typed everything I said into the computer. Neither she nor the detective showed much emotion. It was just a job to them, I guess. Get the kid's confession and move on to the next thing.

When we were done, the policewoman made a printout, and we read it over. It appeared to be everything I had said.

"You need to sign off on it, then," the detective said. He pointed with his stubby finger. "Your name here."

"Go ahead, Brady," Mr. Anderson told me, offering me his pen. "Your full name."

I looked at the space they'd left for my signature and took his pen. *Braden Duvall Parks,* I wrote, feeling every loop and turn of the letters, and wishing, somehow, that I could detach myself from my name.

The detective took the paper, and he and the policewoman left.

Mr. Anderson stayed and sat on the edge of the desk to warn us that a story would undoubtedly appear in the newspaper. "There's going to be a lot of press. Some big headlines."

Sitting in the metal chair in front of him, I kept my hands folded and my head tilted down. It was bad enough already,

but to think everyone in the community would know everything made it worse. My parents would be embarrassed.
And all the kids at school would be shocked. How could I
ever face them again?

My stomach started to knot up—even though I knew this
was the deal.

"Police officers are going to go to each of your friends'
homes now," Mr. Anderson went on. "They'll ask the boys to
come down to the station to talk. They'll read them their
Miranda rights, let them know they have a right to remain
silent and get a lawyer. Then they'll tell them we have the
kayak. That we know what happened because you came
forward."

He waited a second, and I nodded my understanding.

"When they set a date for the trial, Brady, you'll be sub-
poenaed to appear in court as a witness."

I lifted my head and shot him a frightened look.

"I'm afraid so," Mr. Anderson confirmed. "You'll need to
get up in front of them and repeat everything you told us."

I closed my eyes. It felt like someone was squeezing my
chest.

"You've got to be strong, Brady," Mr. Anderson said.

He continued to explain the legal scenario. "Another officer will visit the DiAngelos, and tell them what's going on."

I sucked in my breath, unable to even imagine that. Poor
Mrs. DiAngelo, I thought. She would have to relive it *all over
again*. Only now she would know that I was behind it. That
my very own friends sank the kayak and killed Ben. Maybe
she would even think I was a murderer!

There was a pause when no one said anything. Mr. Anderson clicked his pen shut.

"You're free to go home now," he said quietly. "I need to take care of some paperwork with the state's attorney's office." He turned to my parents. "I'll, ah, need one of you to sign off on a couple things."

Mom offered to go with him. I suspected there were some questions she wanted to ask him out of my earshot. When they opened the door to leave, we could hear telephones ringing and people talking in the outer office. Soon, I thought, the whole world would know.

The door closed again, and silence engulfed the small, cinder-block room. When I looked up, I saw it was just me in the chair and Dad standing by the door, waiting.

God, it was hard to get up out of that chair. It felt like I had hundred-pound weights strapped to my feet. When I did move, finally, I just stood there feeling numb, but very heavy—and completely lost.

Dad came over.

We looked at each other, and Dad said, "You done the right thing today, Brady."

I could have broke down and cried, but I pressed my lips together instead.

Then Dad put his arm around my shoulders, and we walked out together.

CHAPTER TWENTY-FIVE

J.T. and Digger had their initial appearance in juvenile court two days later. I didn't have to go, but I wanted to be there.

Mom had to work because she'd just taken two days off, so it was just Dad and me, and Mr. Anderson, who explained what was happening. I knew that wasn't required of him, and I was glad Carl had recommended him.

We sat in the back of the courtroom before the others arrived, and when Digger and his parents, Mr. and Mrs. Griswald, came in, Mr. Anderson leaned over and asked, "Is that Michael?"

Michael? I looked at him blankly.

Dad said yes for me.

As I soon found out, no one in juvenile court would refer to Digger as Digger—nor even very often by his first name, Michael. Mostly, he was Mr. Griswald. Just as J.T. was Mr. Tyler. Oddly, I found this small slice of protocol comforting.

It was as if a strange and alien part of each of my friends had been involved in sabotaging the kayak.

None of the Griswalds looked back as they took their seats. I'm not sure they knew we were there.

But when J.T. came in with his mother, he glanced our way and did a double take. Our eyes met briefly. J.T. stopped and pursed his lips—then quickly, just once, he nodded.

I sure would like to ask him why I got that nod. He knew I had gone to the police—and after I'd assured him everything would be all right! So why the nod? Was he glad I'd spoken up? Relieved?

Had he been as tortured by it as me?

The double doors at the side of the courtroom opened and closed once more, and a hush fell over the few of us who waited.

"All rise!" a court officer called out when the judge walked in. In juvenile court, the judge is called a master. We stood, and a man sitting in front of us took off his baseball cap as Master Williams in a black robe whooshed out of a little side door at the front of the courtroom, papers tucked under her arm, and strode to the front. She took a couple steps up to a large chair behind a desk built into a tall wooden podium.

Seeing Master Williams for the first time, I had the feeling she was a smart woman. I can't say why. With her short, wavy blond hair tucked behind her ears and wire-rimmed glasses, she reminded me of my fourth-grade teacher. I don't think that's why I thought she was smart, but for some reason I had confidence in her right off.

Both J.T. and Digger stood up and faced her as she spoke. "Jeremy Tyler, Michael Griswald," Master Williams addressed my friends in a clear, direct voice that was neither harsh, nor sympathetic, but somewhere in between. "Do you understand that you are being charged with murder in the second degree in that you did feloniously and with malice aforethought kill and murder Benjamin DiAngelo?"

Murder. Man, it didn't matter how much my parents and Mr. Anderson had prepared me for it, I still couldn't believe they were being charged with *murder!* In my heart I'd hoped for manslaughter, and hearing the word *murder* sent a frozen rod piercing right through the top of my head down into my toes.

I kept watching, straining to see their faces, but I was shut out by their backs. Did they know this was going to be the charge? Neither one of them shook or broke down. Rigidly, they stood there—shocked, I supposed. Probably hating me forever for what I'd done. Maybe hating themselves, too.

"Do you understand you have a right to a lawyer?" Master Williams asked Digger.

When Digger didn't reply, his father stood up behind him. Like Digger, he wore blue jeans and an untucked T-shirt and didn't appear to have shaved or in any other way attempted to spruce up his appearance. "We can't afford no lawyer," he told Master Williams.

"If you cannot afford a lawyer, the court will provide one," Master Williams said.

Mr. Griswald ran a hand over his bald head, but he didn't argue.

Our attorney leaned over to whisper that the Griswalds would be assigned a public defender.

The same procedure happened for J.T., only his mother stood with him and told Master Williams that she would hire her own lawyer.

"That's it, then," Master Williams announced. "I'll see you both back here in thirty days for your adjudication."

Both Dad and I turned to Mr. Anderson.

"That means their trial," he explained, "except there won't be a jury in juvenile court, remember. Master Williams will listen to everyone present their sides then she'll decide the sentence—their disposition."

Adjudication. Disposition. Master. I guess the juvenile court didn't want kids feeling like they were real criminals with a *trial* and a *sentencing* by someone called a *judge*. Even if what got them here in the first place was a criminal act. I didn't laugh, but I shook my head; if you were this deep into it, none of these labels made a lick of difference.

We waited while J.T. and Digger and their families filed out of the courtroom. None of them looked back again. When the room was empty, we stood up and left.

The newspaper reporter, Craig somebody, the guy who interviewed me after I had rescued Ben, called again, but I wouldn't talk to him. He wrote a story anyway. In fact, there were several newspaper stories, including one in the Washington paper, but I didn't read a single one. My parents did.

I heard them shuffling the papers and talking. "It's like a nightmare," Mom complained when she didn't think I was listening.

My mother also cooked up a storm in the first few days after the hearing. All my favorite things: creamed chicken, steak on the grill, fried rockfish, chocolate chip cookies. It wasn't a reward. She was just trying to bolster my mood and keep my spirits up—and maybe my courage, too. But I wasn't very hungry.

Here's the surprising thing: Dad came into my room to talk with me every evening after dinner. "Are you doin' okay?" he'd ask. Or, "Is there anythin' we can do?"

One night, I gathered my strength and asked Dad, "Will you ever forgive me for what I did?"

"Ain't nothin' to forgive," Dad replied. "You didn't do anythin' wrong, Brady. Everybody says things they don't mean. And in the end, you done the right thing, like I tole you."

He took a seat on the end of my bed, where I was already sitting cross-legged, and rubbed his hand over his chin the way he does. "You know, your mother once asked me the same thing, Brady. After she left us that time. I said, 'They ain't nothin' to forgive. Losin' a baby that way—'" He shook his head. "It ain't written down anywhere how to respond to a thing like that. I tole Dee, I said, 'You needed to get away for a while, and then you come back.' Brady, I couldn't fault your mother for that; my love for her runs too deep. Just like it does for you."

My eyes were filling up. "I'm so sorry, Dad."

"I know you are." Dad reached over and touched my knee.

"And I didn't mean for you to have to pay all this money for a lawyer either. I'll bet he's cost a lot, too."

"It's not important, Brady," he tried to put me off.

"Tell me, Dad. How much? I feel like I have a right to know."

He sighed. "Well, he said a flat fee of a thousand dollars. But you know, the money ain't important—"

"The money *is* important," I objected as I reached behind me, under my pillow, for an envelope with $1,200 in it. Carl had driven me to the bank so I could withdraw the money from my account. It was everything I had earned from Mrs. DiAngelo that summer.

"Please, Dad. Take it," I said, offering the envelope.

"No, Brady, I—"

"Please."

I knew the money was gratefully received. My parents needed that money. Why should they suffer because of what my friends and I had done?

But see, even that gesture drove a dilemma through my heart. Because I also felt that I should have given all that money back to Mrs. DiAngelo. True, I wasn't the one who drilled those holes, but I still suffered from the question: *How could I keep anything from Mrs. DiAngelo, after what had been taken from her?*

The weeks between the hearing and the next court date dragged by slower than any doldrums I'd ever encountered.

I forced myself through a couple more books for school and shot a lot of baskets in the side yard. Tried to anyway. Then my cousins from Rhode Island came down with Auntie Janet for a few days. We went into D.C. one afternoon, to the Smithsonian. And Mom took us down to Ocean City for a day at the beach, where we built a sand castle with Emily and jumped around in the waves. At the boardwalk amusement park, Kevin and I rode a few rides and ate funnel cake, but the upcoming court date hung over my head like a dark cloud. And none of the rest of that summer was any fun.

When my relatives were packing up to leave, I asked Auntie Janet if I could give Tiny Tim to Emily. She okayed it right away, and Emily was thrilled. She loved that hamster, while for me, it was just a sad reminder.

During that same time, the juvenile services staff made reports to the court on Digger and J.T. The three of us weren't allowed to see or talk to one another—not that we would have. So, I don't really know what they did those four weeks. I do know that they were both on home detention, which meant they couldn't go anywhere except to a doctor's appointment or their lawyer's office. An electronic bracelet on their ankle monitored their moves. If they went outside a certain radius of their telephone, or tried to take the ankle thing off, the authorities would immediately be notified, and they'd be picked up and put in jail. From what Mr. Anderson said, they even had to shower with that ankle thing on.

But I knew they wouldn't take it off. Mr. Griswald and Mr.

Tyler might have considered removing that ankle bracelet, but not Digger or J.T. And the darnedest thing: I kept remembering something Ben said and I could not get it out of my head.

He said it the afternoon I had baby-sat for him and we watched *The Lion King*. If you've ever seen that movie, you know that toward the end the hyenas turn against the villain, Scar, and attack him. When this happened in the film, Ben had looked up at me and asked, "Why they doing that, Bwady?" I had a mouth full of popcorn, but I told him, "Because he's bad." Well. Ben must have gone on to think about it for a full thirty seconds. "No," he had disagreed, screwing up his little face and shaking his blond hair. I almost forgot what we'd been talking about. "Scaw's not bad," Ben said. "He's just being mean."

CHAPTER TWENTY-SIX

Shoes
Soccer cleats
Office Depot
Haircut

I stared at the list Mom had left under the seagull magnet on our refrigerator. She could scratch the haircut. I'd already had one so I'd look respectable when I raised my right hand and swore to tell the truth, the whole truth, and nothing but the truth. If I were like every other kid in the county, I could have focused on new shoes and school supplies. But three days before I started ninth grade, I went to juvenile court to testify against my two best friends, who had been charged with second-degree murder.

Mom, Dad, and Carl came with me. Mr. Anderson met us at the county courthouse.

It was really hot and humid that day. Stifling. And we

were all encased in formal clothes—Mom in a dress, me in long pants and a sports jacket, with a new tie carefully knotted at my neck. My dad squeezed into a suit that was too tight, and even Carl tucked in a collared shirt. Because the air-conditioning in the old brick courthouse wasn't on or didn't work very well, we all kind of stuck to those wooden benches in the hall where we waited, fanning ourselves with copies of a take-out menu someone had left behind.

But what I remember most about that wait is not the heat and how I was still mustering the courage to stand up in front of everyone and testify without breaking down. No. Mostly I remember feeling scared for J.T. and Digger. Scared and worried about what was going to happen to them.

We were scheduled to start at 9 A.M. At ten minutes of nine someone opened the doors for air, and I could see Digger and J.T. standing on the front steps with their families.

If they saw me, I wouldn't have known. As soon as I spotted them, I kept my eyes averted and spent the rest of the time moving one foot back and forth and staring at a crack in the tile floor. I must have opened and closed my hands and wiped my sweaty palms on my pants a hundred times.

When the courtroom doors inside were unlocked, we went in right away and sat toward the back.

The Griswalds came in after us, and it really struck me how they had spiffed themselves up. Digger wore a nice polo shirt tucked into a pair of clean, belted jeans. Even his father had a suit on, and I know for a fact that was a first for me. Their public defender was a young-looking man with thinning red hair. "I know this guy," Mr. Anderson leaned close to tell us. "He'll do a good job defending Michael."

J.T. came in a minute later wearing a sports coat and a tie, but I'd seen him dressed up before, like on mornings when he'd been to church and we ran into him at the 7-Eleven afterward. His mother was with him, but not his dad. After J.T. took a seat in the front row, I stared at his back. He had a fresh, close-trimmed haircut, which made his ears stick out. I wondered what he was thinking, and if he was scared. I wondered if someday, J.T. and I would ever be friends again.

We rose when Master Williams—"All rise!"—entered. Then we sat down again and listened as a man addressed everyone in court.

"My name is Charles Fine. I'm the state's attorney, and I'm calling the matter of Jeremy Tyler and Michael Griswald, who have been charged with murder in the second degree in the death of Benjamin Anthony DiAngelo. It is my understanding that Mr. Tyler and Mr. Griswald wish to admit to this charge."

A murmur rippled through court.

Surprised and a little confused, Mom, Dad, Carl, and I looked at one another. Mr. Anderson grinned and leaned over from the other side of Dad to tell me, "You're off the hook, Brady. You won't have to testify."

Carl reached across Mom's lap to pat my knee.

It had not occurred to me that this could happen. It threw me.

Master Williams addressed J.T. and Digger. "You admit to this charge? Do you understand this means you plead guilty?"

Digger said, "Yes."

J.T. nodded and mumbled the same.

While I was still reeling from the fact that I didn't have to get up in front of everyone and tell my story, Master Williams was asking J.T. and Digger, "Do you understand that by admitting to this charge, you give up your right to testimony on your own behalf?"

The boys nodded.

"Do you understand that, Mr. Tyler?" Master Williams asked.

"Yes, ma'am," said J.T., his voice barely audible, his head hanging, one hand clasped around the other behind his back.

"Do you understand that, Mr. Griswald?" Master Williams asked.

"Yes," replied Digger, loud and clear. He stood up straight, with his hands at his sides.

I wondered what had come over Digger—*I'll deny it till the day I die!*—in the past month. Why didn't he want to fight it anymore?

"Do you *still* wish to enter a guilty plea?" Master Williams asked again. I guess she wanted to be sure they knew what they were doing.

"Yes, ma'am," J.T. replied.

"I do," said Digger.

"Why?" Master Williams asked them.

The courtroom grew absolutely silent. Everyone's eyes were glued to Digger and J.T.

J.T. spoke first. "Because I did it, Your Honor."

Digger was shaking his head. "No," he said in a pretty loud voice. "I'm the one who's guilty. Not J.T. He didn't want no part of it. He kept watch is all—"

"Mr. Griswald, stop! Please!" Master Williams ordered him.

Digger stared at her, and I could see him take in and let out a big breath.

The judge lowered her voice. "Look," she explained in a kinder voice, "that's not appropriate here. I promise you will have a chance to say whatever you want later. But not now."

She bent her head to write something on the papers in front of her, and attorneys up front started whispering because I guess Digger wasn't supposed to go on like that. But I'd stood up out of my seat, I was so moved by what he said—how he, too, had finally come forth with the truth.

Mom tugged on my jacket, and I sat down. Then we waited a few minutes. I'm not sure why. When Master Williams spoke again, she turned to a man at the side of the courtroom and asked, "Has either of these boys been charged with a crime before?"

"That's the bailiff," Mr. Anderson whispered. "He's got all their background information."

The bailiff replied, "No, Your Honor."

Master Williams went on to ask J.T. and Digger a bunch of questions: how old they were, how much school they'd had, were they under the influence of drugs, alcohol, or medication?

The state's attorney, Mr. Fine, stood up again. He announced that although the DiAngelos were not in court, they had written a "victims' impact statement," which he would read.

Let me tell you, it tore everyone up pretty badly. I heard Mrs. DiAngelo's voice behind every word: "Ben was supposed to start nursery school next month. Now there will be an empty cubby where he would have hung his Winnie-the-Pooh jacket . . . There won't be fingerpaint pictures to hang up on our refrigerator. Or birthday parties to prepare for anymore . . . The tricycle we ordered is still in a box in the basement . . . No more stories in bed . . . There is not a single moment goes by when we don't think of our son . . ."

I bit my bottom lip hard to stop from crying because I knew that the DiAngelos would never get over losing Ben. I knew from losing my baby sister that the pain gets a little less the more time passes, that you go on living, and you learn how to cope with it. But it's like my mom said, even though Amanda died, she'll always be a part of who we are.

At one point, when I covered my eyes with my hand, Mom suggested I leave the courtroom, but I shook my head no and took the Kleenex she offered. She squeezed my hand because she was having as hard a time as I was getting through the DiAngelos' statement. I couldn't see J.T. or Digger's reaction because my head was down the whole time.

When it was over, everyone kind of needed a minute.

I glanced up through watery eyes to see J.T. standing in

front of the judge again. His lawyer, a woman in a bright red suit and with thick, jet-black hair brushing her shoulders, stood with him. She and J.T. didn't look like they belonged together—he was taller than her, for one thing—and I hoped that didn't prove to be bad.

"Your Honor, I would like to begin by pointing out that Jeremy Tyler has never been in trouble with the law before," his lawyer began. "As I'm sure you've read in the reports, he is a good student, a loving son, and a hard worker. Up until sixth grade he was home-schooled by his mother. His grades at school have all been A's and B's. He is active in a youth group at the church he attends with his family, and every day in the summer, he puts in a full eight hours of work on the family's chicken farm."

I felt a twitch in my back. I wanted to jump up and tell everybody that sometimes J.T. hauled out of bed at midnight—or 2 A.M.—and worked clear through the night because those chicken buyers collected around the clock.

"Your Honor," the lawyer went on, "Jeremy was not a willing participant in this criminal act. He felt pressured to help his friend Michael Griswald. Even though Jeremy was present when Michael drilled those holes in the kayak and then replugged them, Jeremy nevertheless believed that the kayak would sink fairly quickly, as a practical joke, forcing Mr. DiAngelo to take a cold swim in to shore. He did worry that they might get caught and have to pay to replace the kayak. But it never occurred to Jeremy that Mrs. DiAngelo and her young son might be the ones to take the boat out first, or that any actual harm would come to anyone."

Of course he didn't want to harm anyone. J.T. had a good heart—the *best!*

"Your Honor, due to the fact that his father is seriously ill and in the hospital, Jeremy is needed at home. And may I remind the court that Jeremy is only thirteen years old. We ask you to please understand that he is still in many ways a child, easily swayed by peer pressure."

It's true! J.T. was just a kid—like *me.* He didn't mean to hurt anyone. I wiped a tear away from the corner of my eye.

"All right, then," Master Williams said. She tilted her head toward Digger.

"Mr. Griswald?"

CHAPTER TWENTY-SEVEN

Digger stood up and jammed his hands in his pockets, then quickly pulled them out and dropped them at his side. But I could see his fingers curl up into nervous fists.

His public defender stood beside him, lifted a legal pad full of notes, and cleared his throat. "Your Honor, Michael Griswald has lived his entire life on the Eastern Shore of Maryland. He is one of five children in his family."

True, I thought. He was one of five, even though his two older brothers had already left home.

"A fair student, Michael is nevertheless a very hard worker," the lawyer continued, "often helping his father, a heavy-equipment operator, to haul loads of gravel and sand. His mother says he is invaluable at home, too, often taking care of his younger brother and sister, including feeding and putting them to bed when both his parents have to work."

He glanced at his notes, and I hoped he would tell everybody in court to look at Digger's chipped tooth, the one in front that never got fixed after he broke it throwing himself on the ice to save my life. *Give him some credit for that,* I wished I could holler. *I wouldn't be here if it weren't for Digger.*

"Michael has never been in trouble with the law before," the lawyer went on. "But his father has had numerous contacts with police. I won't go into detail here, but several complaints have been made against Mr. Griswald for assaulting his wife, often with the children present. Just last month, a restraining order was issued limiting Mr. Griswald's contact with the family."

My eyes shifted to Digger's dad and tried to burn a hole through the back of his thick, bald head, but he sat there like a rock. I wondered if that public defender was going to tell everyone how Mr. Griswald smacked Digger in the eye, too, the night before our Valentine dance in middle school.

"None of this is any excuse for what happened to Benjamin DiAngelo," the young public defender continued, "but I want the court to know that Michael has harbored a lot of resentment and anger toward his father, and has never had a healthy escape valve. Never any counseling of any kind. Never anyone to talk to, or go to for help, except for his grandfather, who recently has become frail and was placed in a nursing home."

At the mention of his grandfather, Digger crossed and then uncrossed his arms.

"I would like to add," the attorney said, "that it was Mr. DiAngelo who purchased the farm belonging to Michael's grandfather, tearing down the old farmhouse before building a new home there. And while we realize this is no excuse for the terrible loss of life that has resulted, we nevertheless ask the court to keep all this in mind. Truly, it was a practical joke gone bad."

The public defender stood back and indicated Digger's mom. "Mrs. Sue Lorraine Griswald would now like to address the court."

Mrs. Griswald, her stringy, gray-streaked hair falling halfway down her back, stood up and tugged a snug blouse over her wide hips. I have always liked Digger's mom. She had a rough life, I know, but she loved telling jokes and teasing the kids when I was around. Sometimes she laughed so hard her eyes would tear up. And I admired her toughness. Maybe she wasn't tough enough to whip Mr. Griswald, but she could drive a dump truck and operate a bulldozer as good as any man.

"I know I have to keep it short," Digger's mom started, "but I wanna tell you, my son, here, is a good boy in his heart. He has always obeyed his parents, and he means the world to Hank and LeeAnn, his little brother and sister. It's true, he does get a fiery temper at times. Runs in the family, I guess . . . Anyways, I can promise you this, that if and when my boy comes home, we will—the children and I—have moved permanent to my sister's over to Denton. She's got a pretty big house on Pea Liquor Road and Digger—that's Michael, Your Honor—he'd go to school there, in Kent County, 'cause I wanna give him a fresh start."

She hung her head for a second and then said, "That's all. I thank you very much for your time, Your Honor."

While she sat down, I watched Mr. Griswald, but he didn't move or even look at his wife.

After that, both J.T. and Digger had a chance to speak for themselves.

J.T. was first, in a voice just loud enough for us to hear: "I am real sorry for what happened to Ben and his family. I wrote the DiAngelos a letter. I told them if I could turn back time, I wouldn't have been there, down at their dock that day. Honestly, we never meant to hurt Ben, or his family. But I know that because of what we did, we hurt them and a lot of other people. I am truly sorry. I know that I will answer to the Lord for this. It is something I will always carry with me."

When J.T. sat down, his lawyer touched him on the shoulder.

Digger scraped back his chair and stood. "I want to say I'm sorry, too," he began. "I've had a long time to think about what we done. And I want Your Honor to know that I'm the only one here who should be blamed. Like my mom said, I get a fiery temper sometimes, and I was pretty angry at Mr. DiAngelo for rippin' down my grampa's house and movin' in there, takin' away all those things in my life that I loved so much. I know now it wasn't Mr. DiAngelo's fault. I was just lashin' out . . . the way my dad lashes out at me, I guess."

Digger paused a moment. I wondered if he was going to go on.

"Anyway, so I told J.T.," Digger continued, "that if he didn't come with me to steal the drill and that glue, that the next time Curtis tried to punch him out at school, I weren't gonna be there to put a stop to it."

Suddenly Digger was turning, his eyes scanning the courtroom until he saw me. "I also want everyone in here to know that my friend Brady Parks—he's sittin' there in the back—that Brady should in no way get blamed or looked down on for what happened. I don't hold nothin' against you, Brady. And I'm sorry I lied to you. We was best friends growin' up and . . . well, you were right, about no one ever forgettin'. That day in the field after school? You asked how I'd feel if it was Hank or LeeAnn in the kayak?"

I sat up tall and nodded so he could see I remembered.

Digger wiped at one eye and turned to his mother. "I don't want nothin' bad to ever happen to the kids, Mom . . . I'm so sorry for all I done to mess things up."

Mrs. Griswald started crying, and when Digger did, too, I couldn't watch any longer.

My head bowed, I listened to him plead with Master Williams. "Please don't punish J.T. the same as me, Your Honor. I brung a lot of shame on him, but I'm the only one here in this room is to blame."

When he finished and sat down, several minutes of silence followed. I felt as though my whole life was on hold right then. I kept looking from the back of J.T. to the back of Digger, and smack out of the blue an oxymoron came to my mind: *alone together*. That's what we were. Together in this room, with all these people, I had never felt more alone.

All this time, Master Williams was busy writing in different folders on her desk. When she finished, she took off her glasses.

"Please stand," the bailiff said quietly.

J.T. and Digger stood.

I knew this was the moment. I felt myself leaning forward, my hands gripping my knees, bracing myself for what she would decide.

She started off slowly. "Mr. Tyler, Mr. Griswald, I appreciate your apologies and all of your heartfelt comments. I know that you have apologized, and I know that you have both said you didn't mean to kill anyone." She paused a second before continuing. "But I'm afraid that in this case, apologies are not enough."

From the corner of my eye I saw Mom fold her hands in her lap. Dad leaned forward beside me.

"What you boys did is like firing a gun into a crowded movie theater just to scare everybody—only someone got killed." Master Williams focused intently on my friends as she explained this. "Mr. Griswald, you've admitted this was all your idea and that you *threatened* your friend, Mr. Tyler, compelling him into committing the act with you."

She turned to J.T. "But, Mr. Tyler, I don't see any evidence here of physical force. You're not a puppet. You could have said no. You could have walked away. But you didn't. And then, you did nothing to *stop* Mr. Griswald. In fact, it is my understanding that you helped to steal that drill and the glue and that you 'stood guard' while Mr. Griswald destroyed property belonging to the DiAngelos, thereby setting the stage for the horrendous act that followed.

"Let this be a lesson to you, Mr. Tyler," she said, "that just because you don't actively participate in a crime, you're not off the hook. No. You are both to blame for what happened to that little boy."

J.T.'s mom put a hand up to her mouth.

"This offense is so serious that there have to be consequences," Master Williams continued, her voice growing harsher. "Look around you. Look at your mothers! Look at the *pain* you have caused your families—not to mention the pain and the enormous loss the DiAngelos have suffered.

"The most important thing you boys need to learn is that what you did was *so reckless* and *so unthinking* that a little boy lost his life. One little boy won't grow up and go to school or ever have a job or a family of his own. Because of what you did." She paused again. "Now, that kind of behavior *cannot* and *will not* go unpunished in the state of Maryland. You need to know this. You need to know this for the rest of your life."

When she finished, she leaned back but continued staring at Digger and J.T. for a moment. Then she put her glasses back on and busily wrote on the papers in front of her.

Both J.T. and Digger looked whipped and stood limply with their heads hanging. It killed me to watch, but I couldn't turn away either, not then.

A couple more minutes went by. Maybe it wasn't even that long.

When Master Williams spoke again, the words came fast. There was some legal jargon, but I grasped this: She committed J.T. and Digger to the custody of juvenile services—to nine months in a forestry camp for juvenile offenders out in western Maryland.

"At the end of nine months, I'll review your records," she

warned. "If I think you haven't learned anything, I will not hesitate to keep you both out there for another couple years."

Nine months. Well, I was relieved, to tell the truth. Nine months was a whole lot better than hearing "until you're twenty-one." Nine months was the school year. By summer, I thought, they could both be home! They could be back in school for sophomore year—well, or freshman year if they had to repeat.

"It's not too bad," Mom said to me.

"No," I agreed.

Everyone was talking in hushed voices, and I began to think that forestry camp had to be better than some juvenile jail place, too.

"They're lucky," Dad noted.

"Damn lucky!" Carl added.

But the next thing we knew, the two sheriff's deputies who had stood quietly at the side of the room all morning were putting handcuffs on my two friends! J.T.'s mother wasn't even allowed to hug him good-bye. The deputy shook his head and gently pushed her arm away even though she was reaching out and calling his name.

"Hey, wait—" I started.

Mom and Dad grabbed my elbows and rushed me out into the hallway then. They got me a drink from the watercooler, and I didn't realize until I took the cup that my hands were shaking.

CHAPTER TWENTY-EIGHT

A "For Sale" sign appeared at the end of the DiAngelos' driveway a few days later. We'd already heard that they moved out. At least they were together, I thought. They were living in Virginia, someone told Mom at work. She also found out that Mrs. DiAngelo would have a baby girl in December.

I still ride my bike by their place once in a while. You can't see the house from the road, of course. But I met a real-estate guy coming out the driveway one day in a black BMW. He stopped to put down his window and say hi. I asked him did he have a buyer yet, and he said, no. So I asked him how the garden was doing. The one by the pool with the rocks and everything.

He smirked. "No garden there anymore."

I had a terrible vision then of Mrs. DiAngelo angrily ripping up the butterfly bush and the flowers I'd planted and heaving them all over the fence.

"She took it with her!" He laughed. "Dug up all those plants, that big purple one, the stones—everything."

"She did?" I guess my mouth hung open after I asked the question.

"Weird, huh?" the guy asked me. "I mean, why not just plant another one? I'll tell ya, I see a lot of strange things, but—"

"No," I stopped him. "It's not weird. See, it was a butter-fly garden. Last spring, we planted it—"

I should have known he wouldn't understand. But before I even had a chance to explain, the guy was buzzing his window up.

Like I said earlier, it's fall now and high school has started. I do my homework and dribble the basketball around. I walk over to the river's edge with Tilly. In fact, on my way there just recently I noticed how the path J.T. and I had tramped down through the soybean field was mostly grown in now, and yet you could still see it, a narrow sandy line between my house and his.

I think a lot about J.T. and Digger. I wonder if they're actually cutting down trees and sleeping in tents at that forestry camp. I wonder if it's cold at night and whether the bugs are bad, and what the food is like and how much they've changed.

I don't suppose I'll ever hear from them again, but Mom says otherwise. Maybe. One day after school, over at the Food Lion in Centreville, I ran into Kate, and she said J.T. was going to write to me. She said he was doing okay, that her dad was still waiting for a new kidney, but that her mom had hired some help at the farm. Kate's hair was up in little braids that were tied with green and white ribbons, my old middle-school colors. She had her field-hockey uniform on and a bag of hamburger rolls in her hand. I wanted to ask her more, but Kate said well, she probably ought to get going. I said, "Me, too."

She looked back, though. When Kate walked off, she looked back.

Dad's still crabbing, but only every other day. Been a bumper crop of crabs these past couple weeks, but it's only because the crabs are on the move now, before winter sets in. Dad lined himself up a good bit of carpentry work for the winter and started in on it early. Still, he says he'll haul out those crab pots again in the spring. I can only hope that I will, too.

Evenings, Dad and I are building us a boat, a little day sailer. We drew up the plans on the kitchen table, then hammered the frames together and laid the keel last night. When it's done, we're going to name it for my mother—she doesn't know it yet—and call it either the *Miss Dee* or the *Miss DeeLight*. I don't know, probably not the latter. Dad said that it made her sound like a porno star or something. He really had me laughing over that one.

I'm sure it'll take us all winter to finish the project, but I look forward to the day we catch our first breeze and go sailing down the Corsica. With any luck, I'll bet we could sail that little boat all the way down to Queenstown and back in one afternoon.

ACKNOWLEDGMENTS

I want to thank the dedicated paramedics of the Annapolis Fire Department's first platoon, especially Lieutenant David Colburn Jr., Lieutenant Larry A. Snyder, and Firefighter Gail Ann Drapeau, for letting me spend time with them. For their generous help with the legal aspects of this story, I wish to thank Cynthia M. Ferris, master of the juvenile court, Anne Arundel County, Maryland, and Assistant State's Attorney Michael Bergeson—as well as attorneys John Hill and Alan Friedman. A special thank-you to waterman Kenny Keen, who took me out on his boat, *Long Shot*; to Tony Everdell, biology teacher at Gunston Day School on the Corsica River; to Bill Goldsborough, senior scientist for the Chesapeake Bay Foundation; and to John Flood, a local conservationist. Finally, I thank my neighbor, Derek Watridge; my sister, Janet Smith; family friend and boatbuilder, Michael Shultz; crackerjack gardener, Barbara Dowling, for her butterfly facts; my always perceptive agent, Ann Tobias; my very thorough editor, Rosanne Lauer; my husband and first reader, John Frece; and my teenage children, William and Hannah, for the details they unwittingly provided.

**Turn the page for a look at
Priscilla Cummings's latest novel,
*The Journey Back***

CHAPTER ONE

BIRTHDAY WISHES

It was my birthday, the day I made up my mind to leave. I'd been thinking seriously about escaping for nearly a week, ever since Visiting Day when Mom showed up and I could see nothing had changed at home. Then, that night, someone peed in my one pair of boots. But that birthday cake was the trigger. It set everything in motion. And by then, I had a plan.

Bet you didn't think losers in prison could actually get a birthday cake, did you? But yeah, we did. The last Friday of each month we celebrated—if you can call it that. In the cafeteria, after evening rec and showers, Mrs. Fielder, our sweaty-faced cook, brought in this big chocolate cake in a pan with white frosting, blue gel writing, sprinkles, a couple candles, the works. I was fourteen years old. What's so pathetic is that it was the first birthday cake I'd had in about eight years. Wouldn't have been half bad, I guess, getting a birthday cake for once, even if I did have to share it with the other September birthdays. But the minute I saw what was written on that cake, my stomach clenched up and my breath caught in my throat—Tio's name was on it, too. Just me and Tio.

"Digger and Tio," Mrs. Fielder announced way too cheerfully. It was creepy hearing our two names strung together like that, but Mrs. Fielder didn't have a clue. Looking rather pleased, she set the cake down on the cafeteria table in front of us while most of the boys, slumped back in their plastic chairs, sang a pitiful version of "Happy Birthday." Some of them didn't sing at all, and even those who did, you could tell no one had his heart in it. They just wanted to get it over with so they could eat cake, which we would all agree is far better than half a baloney sandwich on dry bread and rancid fruit juice for our evening snack. Their voices rose with a tad more enthusiasm toward the end—*Digger and Teeeee-ooooooo*—while my head spun like crazy because the bottom line was this: my name was written *above* Tio's on that cake, which meant things would come to a head fast.

"Digger, go ahead and make a wish," Mr. Rankin said. If I had to pick one, Mr. R. was probably my favorite counselor. He set his beefy hands on his hips and, as he caught my eyes, smiled kindly and nodded once. We'd had a talk that afternoon about "if/then thinking"—you know, if you do this, then that might happen—and he was probably hopeful some of it sank in. "Blow out one candle," he instructed. "Then let Tio blow out the other one."

I knew this was a test and I had to make up my mind quickly. I could breathe slow, count backward from ten, try to go with the flow. But I was burning inside because I still wasn't over the humiliation of walking around in those damp, stinky boots a week ago. Ever tried to clean urine out of your shoes with a Kleenex? Let me tell you, it doesn't work very well. Everywhere I went, I stunk up the place. At least I knew who was behind it. My eyes flicked over to Tio and back. Unsmiling, he sat up stiffly, his chin up, his eyes narrowed, and rested his tattooed hands on the table directly across from me. No way was he going to accept seeing my name above his on that cake. That's how small and mean he was. Maybe it was 'cause of his half-a-brain gang mentality. I don't know, and frankly, I don't care.

Still, I swallowed hard. All the other boys were quiet but perked up by then, scraping their chairs back and leaning forward, watching me like hawks. They were waiting to see what I'd do 'cause with my hesitation and all, everyone could feel the tension.

"Go ahead," Mr. Rankin urged gently, and I glanced at him again, hoping that brief look could say what I couldn't: that I didn't hold nothing against my counselors and I hated to disappoint them. Mr. R. and Miss Laurie, the mental health lady, they tried hard to set me straight. It wasn't their fault I couldn't change. I was doing what I had to do, which was get one up on Tio before he got one up on me. And then get the hell out of there and make it home in time to protect my mom and my little brother and sister.

I stood up and, while staring down at the cake, drew in a chest full of stale cafeteria air that still smelled like canned corn from dinner. Quickly, I wished to myself that Tio—and my father—would die miserable deaths; then I leaned forward and blew both of those candles out.

Stone silence.

"Sorry," I said softly, pulling my shoulders back while two tiny wisps of smoke drifted away. I shrugged and looked at Tio. The slightest hint of a smile may have crept on to my lips. "Looks like you don't get no birthday wish."

It worked.

Tio jumped up out of his chair so fast he knocked it over behind him. The little car thief may be short, but he was fast. In a flash, he lunged forward, picked up the cake with both hands, and threw it at me hard. I jumped back on my toes, and to the side quick, like a batter avoiding a fastball, low and inside, as the cake whizzed by. It hit a kid named Jimmy smack in the chest, then slid down the front of him, leaving a huge ski trail of frosting on his sweatshirt. He stood up, spreading out his arms, like *what the heck?* And the pan clattered to the floor.